My Bad Decisions

Special Edition

On my Own

Carrie Ann Ryan

My Bad Decisions

An On My Own Novel

By
Carrie Ann Ryan

My Bad Decisions
An On My Own Novel
By: Carrie Ann Ryan

Cover Art by Wildfire Designs

Praise for Carrie Ann Ryan

"One of the best family romance series around! Carrie Ann Ryan brings the heat, emotions, and love in each story!" ~ NYT Bestselling Author Corinne Michaels

"Count on Carrie Ann Ryan for emotional, sexy, character driven stories that capture your heart!" – Carly Phillips, NY Times bestselling author

"Carrie Ann Ryan's romances are my newest addiction! The emotion in her books captures me from the very beginning. The hope and healing hold me close until the end. These love stories will simply sweep you away." ~ NYT Bestselling Author Deveny Perry

"Carrie Ann Ryan writes the perfect balance of sweet and heat ensuring every story feeds the soul." - Audrey Carlan, #1 New York Times Bestselling Author

"Carrie Ann Ryan never fails to draw readers in with passion, raw sensuality, and characters that pop off the page. Any book by Carrie Ann is an absolute treat." – New York Times Bestselling Author J. Kenner

"Carrie Ann Ryan knows how to pull your heart-strings and make your pulse pound! Her wonderful Redwood Pack series will draw you in and keep you reading long into the night. I can't wait to see what comes next with the new generation, the Talons. Keep them coming, Carrie Ann!" –Lara Adrian, New York Times bestselling author of CRAVE THE NIGHT

"With snarky humor, sizzling love scenes, and brilliant, imaginative worldbuilding, The Dante's Circle series reads as if Carrie Ann Ryan peeked at my personal wish list!" – NYT Bestselling Author, Larissa Ione

"Carrie Ann Ryan writes sexy shifters in a world full of passionate happily-ever-afters." – *New York Times* Bestselling Author Vivian Arend

"Carrie Ann's books are sexy with characters you can't help but love from page one. They are heat and heart blended to perfection." *New York Times* Bestselling Author Jayne Rylon

Carrie Ann Ryan's books are wickedly funny and deliciously hot, with plenty of twists to keep you guessing. They'll keep you up all night!" USA Today Bestselling Author Cari Quinn

"Once again, Carrie Ann Ryan knocks the Dante's Circle series out of the park. The queen of hot, sexy, enthralling paranormal romance, Carrie Ann is an author not to miss!" *New York Times* bestselling Author Marie Harte

My Bad Decisions

The first time he kissed me, we kept it a secret.

Tanner and I have been at each other's throats ever since.

The second time he kissed me, I told myself not to fall.

I should have known something burned beneath the surface and I couldn't resist him.

The third time led to something more and now one positive test later, neither one of us can walk away.

Only when his past sheds light on every difference we've chosen to ignore, we'll have to fight for each other, or lose everything before we've even had a chance.

ONE

Natalie

I had grown up in a world of privilege. High teas, boarding schools, Mercedes as starter cars before teenagers got their even higher-end vehicles, and scary amounts of entitlement.

My parents had done their best not to spoil me, and I thought I had some concept of reality. At least, that's what I told myself.

I did not have an Ivy League education, but I could have gone to any school I set my eyes on. Money was no object, and with the multiple trust funds that had come to me when I hit twenty-one, I didn't even need a job. My grandmother had even suggested that I go to school to get my MRS degree—aka a husband—not my BA, BS, or Ph.D.

No, a Blake did not need a college degree, especially if that Blake happened to be a woman.

Now, if I had been born with a penis, that would have meant a whole other set of rules, requirements, and expectations. I would have had to go to business school—especially the Ivy League ones—and perhaps even law school. Some were doctors, but most of my cousins and extended family were lawyers or business executives that knew how to work with money and how to make more of it.

That was what Blakes had done for generations.

If you asked my grandmother, the Blakes came in on the Mayflower. I wasn't quite sure if that was true, though my grandmother probably had the papers to prove it—forged or not.

I was not the Blake my grandmother hoped for, but at least I could look at myself in the mirror. Grandmother lived on the east coast, well away from us, and I rarely saw her since she didn't like to travel to Colorado. But her mouthpiece, my mother, made sure her rules were clear.

My school friends had been of the same ideals as my grandmother, the same background as me before I decided to go to Denver State University for a degree in social work and not one of the premier colleges. I had been part of the crowd that stuck up their noses and had lunches that were a little more liquid than they were sandwich-based—even at my age. I'd never truly fit in, but I had tried to find my way with them before I changed my mind about who I wanted to be.

With all of that in mind, it honestly surprised me that the location for this bachelorette party was not some high-society tea or something my grandmother would approve of. Of course, the name of the club we were about to enter might seem decent—at least from the outside—but I didn't think it fit with the usual routine.

After all, the *Executive Gentlemen's Club* was not necessarily for the Blake gentlemen.

No, this would be something far different.

"Okay, girls, everyone have their dollar bills?" Janice asked as she held up her Chanel wallet purse.

Victoria, Samantha, Charli, and Karen all giggled, holding up their equally pristine bags. I held back a sigh and tugged my crossbody Dior bag a little closer.

"I don't see happiness on your face," Janice stated as she narrowed her eyes at me. "Natalie, come on. We're near your side of town. You should enjoy yourself."

The other girls giggled and whispered to each other, and I just rolled my eyes. Somehow, I was friends with these rich bitches—as Tanner would've called them—and I wasn't sure how.

Why had I thought of Tanner just then? Why could I clearly hear his voice when I shouldn't.

Tanner was a sort-of friend of mine that I had become close to over the past two years. Especially since his roommates were dating every one of *my* roommates.

Somehow, three of the guys and three of the girls had ended up together and would probably get married sometime soon. However, Nessa and Miles were still in the budding phase of their relationship and hadn't declared their feelings for one another. My grandmother would somewhat approve of the girls getting their MRSs, even though they were all going towards graduate schools for other degrees. Only Grandmother wouldn't dwell on those other letters some would eventually get behind their names.

It was the three letters up front that mattered.

The idea that I still hadn't had a serious relationship, even with all the eligible men my mother tried to set me up with, was not something I needed to dwell on.

Nor was Tanner's voice in my head.

"It's my bachelorette party," Victoria said, clapping her hands in front of her. She had a hundred-dollar manicure on those nails, a four-hundred-dollar haircut, and a four-figure bag in that hand of hers.

She looked gorgeous—they all did—yet I felt like I was miles away from them. Holding back a sigh, I realized I just needed to get through the night and try to remember that I used to be friends with these people.

Even though I wasn't the same Natalie Blake I had been when I left high school.

"I promise, we'll have fun. Though I wasn't expecting a male revue strip club as our evening's activities."

"We've already had the champagne and appetizers. Now, we're going to the buffet," Samantha added as she giggled into her clutch.

I held back an eye roll as the others giggled with her, and we made our way to the front of the line. Yes, there was an actual red-velvet-roped line to get into the place. I hadn't realized male revues were so popular in Colorado. Though we *were* near downtown Denver and two large universities. Perhaps this was what people did in their evenings when they weren't going to school or having house parties.

I needed to get out more. Although I wasn't exactly sure what I would get into tonight.

Hopefully, nothing. I did not want to be scarred for the rest of my life. Images of men in tight leather randomly gyrating to music from the late '90s filled my mind, and I tried to push that out of my brain.

I was a big proponent of doing what worked for a person. If you wanted to strip for money, I said go for it. If you wanted to take off your clothes and enjoy yourself, then have fun.

I just didn't want to be here for it since I had no idea what I was supposed to do.

I knew with complete certainty that I was the only virgin in the group—just like I was the only virgin in most groups.

I held back a painful and hollow laugh, thinking of another friend who used to joke with me about being the last virgin. But I had lost Corinne over a year ago now, and there was no bringing her back.

"Now you're truly frowning," Janice tittered, glaring at me. "If you don't get those wrinkles away from your forehead, you're going to need more Botox than any of us."

I sighed, put a bright smile on my face that I knew looked a little manic but was necessary to fit in with this crowd, and rolled back my shoulders. "I'm ready. Bring on whatever the hell we're getting into."

"The language. I guess that's what comes when you go to a state university," Karen muttered to herself as we walked in. I ignored her and noticed a few of the people in line glaring at us. I wondered what strings they'd pulled to get into the VIP section and to the head of the line for a male strip club.

We walked past a large bouncer, who swept his gaze over all of us, but I didn't know if it was to check us out or to see if we had any weapons or extra body glitter. I held back a snort at that and told myself not to be a party pooper. I needed to have fun tonight. Maybe let loose. Only the people that I wanted to let loose with were all out on dates tonight.

My roommate Nessa was on a date with Miles, and I thought the relationship might be going well. I was worried about the rest of the semester with everything Nessa was going through, but things seemed to be progressing nicely with Miles. Nessa hadn't said that she loved him yet, but I knew it. I might be a virgin, but I was a romantic at heart.

Dillon, Elise, Pacey, and Mackenzie were out on a double date. I thought it was cute that the four of them were spending so much time together, and I had a feeling those bonds would last forever.

I wasn't sure where my bonds would end up because I always felt like I was on the outside looking in. That didn't seem right, and I needed to be better about it. Still, it felt that way sometimes.

I blinked myself out of my thoughts and looked around at the leather-adorned interior of the club and the red velvet ceiling. It was nice in here. It didn't smell like smoke or sweat or other bodily fluids, and there was a decent bar. Still, I had no idea what to expect. There were corner tables all around, as well as some in the middle. Groups of people mingled: businessmen, businesswomen, college-aged people. *Everyone.*

I nearly tripped as I looked over and recognized another student from my class. Their name was Tru, without the *e*. They waved and winked before gesturing towards the stage. A very built man wearing a firefighter costume gyrated, and I squinted, wondering how I could have missed *that* part of his costume.

I blushed, scampered after my friends, and gave Tru a little wave. They rolled their eyes, leaned into their friends, and the group in rainbow-colored attire and enormous wigs waved back.

I knew that Janice and the others would get angry if I left them, even for a minute, but I would deal with it. I walked up to Tru and hugged them hard.

"Hey, you. This is the last place I thought I would see *the* Natalie Blake."

I winced and hugged them again. "Bachelorette party. For a friend from high school. I haven't seen them in over a year, so I'm a little bit out of my element in more ways than one." I didn't mean to sound so bitter about that, but it was true. Everyone else in the group had gone to the same school, and most of them were married—everybody but Victoria and me.

Victoria was getting married next week, though. I would be the lone old maid in the group. I would turn twenty-two next month. I really was the old maid. Lovely.

Tru gave the girls a look, held back the eyebrow raise I knew they wanted to give me, and gestured towards their group.

"My friends, this is Natalie, a friend from class." They turned to me again. "We're here for a bachelor party of our own for Brandon and Franklin," they said, gesturing to the others at the end of the table, both with frilly white sashes, large beards, and tiaras. They looked *amazing*.

"It's nice to meet you all."

Tru introduced me to the rest of the group and asked me if I wanted to sit for a drink.

"I should probably return to the group I came with because I am here for a bachelorette party."

"Considering that one of them is glaring daggers at you, you're probably not wrong," Franklin said. "Thank you for the congratulations. And if you need a place to hide, we're here for you. It's always a safe place with us."

I smiled widely and hugged Tru again. "I don't know the etiquette at a strip club, but can I send over a drink? Or maybe a lap dance?" I said with a laugh. Everybody joined in, thankfully.

"Look at you. Again. I wouldn't have thought those words would come out of your mouth."

I shoved playfully at Tru's shoulder. "Be nice. I have no idea what I'm doing."

"Clearly. But we love you anyway. You're welcome to send over a drink. The lap dance…not so much because we're a little territorial," Tru added with a grin. I smiled, said my goodbyes, and took a little extra time handing over a fifty to their waiter. The waiter smiled and went over to the booth, and I made my way back to the girls.

"What were you doing with them?" Victoria asked. I narrowed my eyes, ready to defend my friends, but she held up a hand. "Not because they seem to be having a lovely gay bachelor party, but because you were with our group, not them. We may be bitches, but we're not bigoted bitches. Duh." She held up her martini glass. "Now, sit and enjoy the show."

Relief spread through me, and I was grateful that she had just come right out and said it. She was right. They were bitches and proud of it, but they only judged people for their money and class—or lack thereof—not anything else. And that was a horrible thing to think about my former friends.

I sat down at the end of the booth and looked at

the sparkly pink drink in front of me. Karen leaned over. "It's a sparkling rosé with strawberries. Sounded good."

"It looks tempting. Thank you." The others held up their half-empty glasses, and we clinked and said our cheers. I took a drink of my sweet and sparkly concoction.

We were taking the limo home, so I could have as much as I wanted, but I wasn't in the mood to drink tonight. Everybody seemed as if they were having fun, and I felt like I was two steps behind.

A voice came over the speaker, and I instinctively looked towards the stage. "And now, the moment you've all been waiting for. It's time to tame this bad boy. He may be wearing leather, and he may have a few chains waiting for you behind these curtains, but… here we go. Let's see what he has in those hips tonight."

I winced as the girls screeched when a younger man with dark hair he'd brushed back slid onto the stage. He wore jeans with holes in the knees, a leather jacket, and a white T-shirt. He moved those hips so sensually, I couldn't help but be drawn to them. I swallowed hard, wondering why I cared about this guy's hips and not the firefighter's—or his hose attachment.

"Look at him. Look at that bad boy from the

wrong side of the tracks," Samantha joked. "I wouldn't mind figuring out exactly how bad he can be."

"I know, right? Just a fling. Of course, my flings are over," Victoria said, and I looked over as she wiggled her finger with her four-carat diamond ring.

I pulled my gaze from her and ignored how they continued talking about the bad boy from the wrong side of the tracks. They had no idea who this person was. They shouldn't be talking bad about him, and I didn't want to hear what they thought of him.

He moved his hips and slowly stripped off his leather jacket—to the delighted squeals and shouts of the crowd. He worked the music, getting low to the ground and grinding, but the shadows were above his face, and I couldn't see any details.

Those arm muscles as he stripped off his shirt, though? Whoa. Dear, God. And that back of his was all broad muscle, too.

He was gorgeous. I couldn't help but blush, yet I knew this was wrong. Ogling him. I shouldn't be enjoying this. But I was a warm-blooded woman. Maybe I could have just a little fun. I let out a squeal with the rest of them, wanting to join in. And then he turned.

I stiffened, met his gaze for an instant, and all breath rushed out of me. This wasn't happening. It couldn't be. I had to be seeing things. After all, I'd never been to a strip club before. Surely, the first one I went to wouldn't have a stripper I recognized.

He didn't seem to care when our eyes met. Instead, Tanner moved his hips and put one hand on his belt.

I swallowed hard, watching how his thumb swiped at the button of his jeans, first one and then another. I realized I hadn't known men still wore button fly jeans.

I couldn't breathe.

Tanner Hagen, the final roommate, my somewhat friend and somewhat nemesis, was currently stripping at my friend's bachelorette party.

This was what death and mortification truly felt like.

My cheeks flamed, and I took a big swallow of my drink, nearly choking on it. "I have to use the bathroom." The girls waved me off, not caring about my crudeness.

I nearly tripped over my heels as I made my way down the hallway and past another bouncer. "You going to hurl?" the bouncer asked.

I shook my head, my cheeks red. "I just need some air. Can I go out this back door?"

"No problem. You got your ticket?"

I held up my hand and waved it so his gaze went to the glowing wristband that served as the ticket. "Jeff out there will let you in when you're ready. Just breathe. Take care of yourself."

"Thanks," I said, warmed by his care.

"You're welcome. You won't be alone out there. He'll keep you safe."

I stumbled out the back door, nodded at the other bouncer, took a few more steps, and then put my back to the brick. I sucked in a deep breath of the cool air and let out another. I couldn't focus. I couldn't do anything.

Tanner was a stripper?

I knew he worked late and long hours to pay for school and other things, but I didn't know he was a *stripper*. Did anyone else?

No, they would have told me. Or…maybe not. It was none of my business. Hadn't I just said that people were allowed to do whatever they needed to pay for school?

Tanner, though… The man who had starred in more than one of my fantasies was a stripper.

And he was even sexier in person than he was in my dreams.

All hard ridges, dark hair, and light eyes. He had a smattering of chest hair that glistened under the lights, but he was mostly all sweat-slick skin and rigid muscles, with a little trail of hair down from his belly button into those jeans I hadn't looked too closely at because I had run before he fully pulled them off.

This wasn't a nude strip club, so he'd likely be

wearing a G-string or briefs or whatever under them. But the girls would see nearly *everything*—as would Tru and their friends.

Everyone would see him moving those hips and everything else, and I had run.

Sad, little virgin Natalie had run from Tanner and his penis.

That needed to be the title of my new diary entry this evening. I put my hands over my face and let out a deep breath, freezing at the sound of gravel underfoot.

"So. Here we are."

I looked up at him, letting my hands fall to my hips as I coughed. "You're wearing clothes."

That wasn't exactly what I had wanted to say, but I couldn't take it back now.

He quirked a smile, giving me that damn sexy look of his that I both hated and loved all at once. I didn't dislike Tanner. He was nice and sweet most of the time. He cared for everyone in his circle, but he also had secrets, pushed people away, and was growly and judgy when in a mood.

Perhaps now, I understood why he held some things close to the vest. But that didn't mean I had to like it.

"I didn't think I'd see Natalie Blake here."

I wasn't sure if I liked him saying my name like

that, even though I really *did* like that he said my name like that.

"I'm here for a bachelorette party."

"Didn't realize one of our friends was getting married," he drawled as he came forward. He wore those same jeans and white T-shirt, but the leather jacket was long gone.

How long had I been standing out here trying to cool down?

Long enough for him to finish his set and come out here fully dressed, apparently.

"They're friends from high school. Not truly my friends anymore, but they asked me to come, so I did."

He tilted his head, stared at me, and then put a hand against the brick wall on either side of my head. I was caged, trapped. Yet I didn't want to push him away.

I'd only had that single glass of champagne. But, apparently, it had gone right to my head.

"Don't tell them, Natalie."

I tilted my head, studying the angle of his jaw. I knew he wasn't talking about my high school friends anymore. "Of course, I won't."

He leaned closer, his lips a bare breath from mine. "Again?" he asked, his voice low, a growl in his tone.

I swallowed hard, my gaze going to his lips. "We can't."

He smirked. "Why? Because I'm a poor stripper?"

Hurt sliced through me, and I leaned forward, brushing his hair from his forehead. He radiated heat, and his gaze was full of something I couldn't read. Still, he looked *so* damn good. "No, because you don't like me."

"Of course, I do, princess."

Then he pressed his lips to mine, and I told myself—once again—that this would be the last time I kissed Tanner Hagen.

Two

Tanner

"Thank you so much, Tanner," my mom said from my side as she knelt next to the open cabinet door. I was currently lying on my back, wrench in hand, and my head below the pipes in my mother's kitchen, trying to decide if I could figure this clog out on my own.

I should be able to. After all, I'd had to fix it a few times already. But I knew that, one day soon, my mother would have to call an actual plumber.

"It's no problem, Mom. Just make sure Cody stops throwing food down here."

"I know, I know. For a kid who's never had a garbage disposal, I feel like he got used to them by watching fancy kitchen shows on TV or something."

I snorted, smiling even though my mother couldn't see my face.

"Kids these days. Some watch violence, some learn about fancy kitchens with garbage disposals."

"Next, he'll want an ice maker." The sound of her voice made me laugh, and I took a second to let the rumbles in my chest calm before I went back to securing the pipe.

"The clog's fixed. At least here and for now. You know, you may need to replace a few things soon, right?" I asked, and Mom sighed.

"I know. And I know you want to be an architect not a plumber, but I'm glad you learned a few of those skills during that one summer job. Are you enjoying your new job? With the agency?"

My mother thought I worked for an architectural firm as a paid intern. That couldn't be further from the truth. But it wasn't like I could tell my mother that I was a stripper. I took off my clothes for money. But somebody needed to. My mom worked full-time as an elementary school teacher, and with her income, she barely kept a roof over her head. I wasn't sure how much longer she could. The military still paid out benefits for my dad, but there weren't that many. When

I was younger, an IED blast overseas had changed our world. Losing my father had rocked our family to its core and forced my mother to become a completely different person.

She had pretty much raised us alone since Dad was rarely around because of deployment. However, it wasn't his fault. The military had taken him around the world, and he'd fought for our country. He'd helped others but then died before he even got his first gray hair.

Leaving behind my mother, me as a surly teen, and Cody, my far younger brother.

We were finding our way. While it sometimes didn't feel like we were, we *were* making it work.

The bottom line was, a teacher's salary plus a widow's benefit didn't add up to much. That meant I needed to send money back to my mom to help out where I could. Raising kids was expensive, and Cody needed a normal life.

So, if I had to take off my clothes to music and gyrate for cash, I would. Soon, I wouldn't have to. Of course, there were routine medical bills and life that needed to be taken care of, too.

One day soon, I *would* work as a paid intern while finishing up my schooling and then get a job that didn't include body glitter and random booty shorts.

I wasn't a huge fan of G-strings, so the booty shorts were it for me.

The idea that that was part of my daily choices should have concerned me. But at this point, I didn't care.

"Seriously, thank you again, Tanner darling. Can you stay for dinner?"

I gave her a look, and she cringed. I hated seeing that expression on her face, so I leaned up and kissed her on the cheek. "I have some studying to do, and I promised I would meet the guys later for dinner. We're all so busy; we don't get to spend a lot of time together."

"I feel like that's my line. And you don't have to go. It's not that bad, Tanner."

I refrained from saying anything.

Of course, fate hated me, and it seemed I wasn't going to be able to escape as quickly as I wanted to.

The screen door slammed open, and a deep voice bellowed from the front door. "Isabella, get me a beer, won't you? Today's been a shit day."

"Of course, Jared. I'll be right there."

"That's my babe. You know exactly what I want."

My mother blushed, and I pinched the bridge of my nose, willing myself not to growl.

The fact that my mother was dating wasn't the

issue. I wanted her to be happy. Dad had died a while ago, and Mom deserved a life full of love and everything she wanted.

That she was dating *Jared*, my dad's former friend—and a complete asshole—was. It really wasn't what I had imagined when she had said that she might want to start dating again.

Jared had shown up for the funeral and hadn't left. At first, he'd started as the kind and caring friend who ordered my mother around as a way to *help*. Then he'd become the guy who moved in, though I wasn't sure exactly how that had happened.

I had moved out as quickly as I could, not wanting to stay under the same roof as Jared, but I hated leaving my mother and Cody behind. However, it was either leave or go to jail for murder. Given the way Jared and I fought, one day, it likely *would* have been murder. I would have killed the bastard. Wrapped my hands around that thick neck of his and never let go.

I hated how he treated my mother. Like she was staff. And the way he degraded my little brother for not liking sports or anything so-called *manly*.

Whenever I said something or tried to step up, my mother broke down just a little bit more. I hated it.

One day soon, Cody would come out to Jared, and I wasn't sure what would happen then. I didn't care what Jared did to me, but if he hurt my little brother? I *would* kill him.

My mother seemed to realize that, so she did her best to ease the tension between us—but that wouldn't happen.

I cleaned up what I had been working on and turned on the water to wash my hands when Jared walked in.

"I said I'd deal with that, Isabella. No need to bring in the boy," he growled. He wrapped his hand around the back of my mother's neck and kissed her hard. She didn't back away and didn't look as if she hated it, so I didn't say anything.

Images of me ripping Jared's head off for how he manhandled her filled my brain.

"You done, boy?" Jared asked.

"Not a boy. And I pretty much am. The clog's fixed." Jared should have been able to do it himself, as it wasn't that hard of a thing, but God forbid he get his hands dirty for anything other than playing with his dick.

"We'll see. We'll see. You headed out?" he asked, and I knew it wasn't a question. I would be leaving, or Jared would make me.

"Boys." Isabella wrung her hands in front of her. My mother was not a weak woman. She had raised two of us, practically by herself, and had dealt with the unending blow of losing my father. She had lifted her chin and continued to live—though she hadn't thrived.

As soon as Jared walked in, I saw her shoulders hunch. She became a different person. Nothing I could say would fix that. She wouldn't let me.

I hated Jared.

"I'm headed out, Mom. Love you." I kissed her on the cheek, watched how Jared's eyes narrowed at that, and then grabbed my things.

"Will we see you this weekend for dinner?" she asked, and I heard Jared muttering, rooting around in the fridge behind her.

"I've got work and class and schoolwork to deal with. I'll call, okay? I want to see Cody."

"Of course. I love you." I leaned down, hugged her close, and inhaled the light perfume she always wore that reminded me of home.

"Just let me know if you need anything," I added.

"I've got her. She's not going to need anything from you, boy."

I glared over my mom's head at Jared, and his hands fisted at his sides as he took a step forward. My mother patted my chest and gently pushed me away.

She could have outright slapped me, and it would have hurt less. There was nothing I could do. She was happy. Jared didn't hurt her. He just hated me.

I nodded at them both and then headed out to my

truck. It was old and a little battered, but it got me through.

If I hadn't had to send money back home or use it to pay for my astronomically expensive schooling, then perhaps I'd be able to afford a better truck, considering what I made while stripping.

However, the money didn't stay with me.

I pulled onto the highway, dealt with the five o'clock traffic, and cursed myself. I hadn't been thinking. I should have taken the side roads, but here I was, my anger mounting with each passing moment, sitting on the highway and letting my truck overheat even in the chilly weather.

Denver traffic was horrendous, and no matter what I did, I-25 at any corridor was Satan's playhouse.

I pulled into the driveway and noticed mine was the only vehicle here. The guys were either at work or out, and I was a little grateful for that. Anger rode me. And, frankly, I felt a little mean right now. It was as if Jared's nastiness rubbed off on me every time I was over there. I just needed to flick it off before I dealt with my roommates.

I hadn't seen any of them since I'd run into Natalie at the club the night before, and I honestly wasn't sure what to do if they saw me, and I realized they knew.

I shouldn't be ashamed of what I did. It paid the bills, and a lot of people were strippers. Yet my friends didn't need to strip for money to pay for their schooling. They had honest, hardworking jobs that didn't have anything to do with the way they shook their hips or how their dicks filled out their booty shorts.

No, they all worked hard and didn't have to be me. Didn't have to do what I did.

I didn't know why, but I hated myself just a little bit more because of that.

While I wanted to trust that Natalie wouldn't tell them what she had seen—after all, she hadn't told them about anything between us before—I was still worried.

Now that one person knew, everyone else might know, too. Wasn't that the way it always worked? It was hard to keep secrets in our small group.

I made my way into the kitchen and frowned at the note on the fridge.

It wasn't addressed to me per se, but it was still a to-do list.

Not things needing handyman skills in our house, considering Pacey's family owned it, and he took care of it. No, this was for the girls' house. Their landlord was a piece of shit and never took care of anything.

Anger mounting, I took the to-do list from the fridge and figured that since I already had my tools out, I should just deal with it.

Maybe Natalie would be there, and I could make sure she kept her mouth shut.

Or perhaps I could get my mouth on hers again.

I cursed at myself and headed to my truck. I *could* walk there, but I had more tools in the bed, so I would just deal with parking near their place.

I had a key to their house, just like all the girls had access to ours. Honestly, it was becoming a little too *Brady Bunch* for me, given how things kept overlapping. However, everyone was seeing one another, so I guessed it made sense.

As for Natalie and me? A few stolen kisses and some glances when no one was looking? That didn't mean much.

She just wanted to cross those train tracks and figure out what it felt like on the other side. Maybe I would let her do it. Just to see.

It wasn't fair that Natalie constantly filled my dreams and made my dick so hard it was difficult to walk in the mornings.

No, I wouldn't think too hard about her. Instead, I would fix her damn house, make sure she kept her mouth shut, and pretend that I didn't want her more than my next breath.

I knew who I was. I was the kid with no money, a shady past, and one who took his clothes off for a living.

I didn't get the privileged princess—the one with the fancy bags and the nice car.

Natalie was all high teas, fancy lunches, and staff.

I was the guy she'd have to hide.

So, she wasn't for me.

Even if she made my mouth water.

THREE

Natalie

My head hurt, but I only had myself to blame. I had told my mother that I didn't have time to do lunch with them this afternoon as I had a paper due in two days, multiple books to read, and was only halfway through. However, a Blake always made time for others. And they always made time for family.

So, when my mother told me to come to lunch, even if I didn't have time, I did. I jumped when she said jump.

It hadn't helped that lunch hadn't been exactly

what I had planned. No, it had turned into a matchmaking session. Again.

If I did my calculations right, I had now met every available son in my parents' social circle. I had even met a few daughters because my parents were open to whatever choice I made, as long as I made a choice. Having to explain to my mother that I did not have time to date, and that while the people they introduced me to had been lovely in most cases, I wasn't going to marry them and make my mother proud was always hard.

It wasn't that she wanted me to get merely an MRS. She wanted me to get a degree to be proficient with my MRS.

You would think it was the 1950s instead of the twenty-first century.

However, I couldn't do anything about what my mother wanted. She would figure it out eventually. Realize that I wasn't going to walk away from the job I wanted to get. That I wouldn't walk away from social work.

It would be hard and grueling, and while I was grateful for the trust funds I had, that privilege wouldn't be the only thing I relied on.

It would be nice to find someone, though. Someone to share that time with. To share the burdens and happiness. To fall in love with.

My friends had all done that. They had found their happiness and their forevers, even if nobody was engaged yet in my group. It would come. I knew it, deep down from the bottom of my heart—even if Nessa and Miles were only moments into their relationship and hadn't yet declared themselves.

I wanted to fall in love, get married, and have children. I wanted to have that life. But I hadn't found my person yet.

I hadn't even had sex yet, which honestly was the bane of my existence. I wished I could just get it over with and have fun. That way, it wouldn't be this heavy weight on my shoulders, a label that I kept putting on myself even if I didn't want to think about it. I didn't mean to end up a virgin at my age. It had just happened. I had dated a boy at the beginning of high school, and it hadn't ended well, to say the least. I had even dated a girl my junior year. Heather had been sweet and kind, but we hadn't fit.

I had gone on a few dates in college, even more if you counted the family dates my mother kept forcing me on at lunches like today's, but nothing had clicked.

The only person I ever felt any kind of pull towards was probably the last person I should. He was the final roommate, and even though we would complete a fabulous matching set in some people's eyes, it was something I couldn't do because dating Tanner would lead to *so* many bad decisions. Not because of who he was, but because he was intoxicating, and I knew I could become addicted if I weren't careful.

If I gave in, what would happen when he walked away?

He would have to walk away because he had plans and was working so hard towards them. This late in the game, I would only be a distraction, so that's what I kept telling myself.

I pulled into my garage and noticed that the other girls weren't here yet. I didn't know their schedules for the day, but I could probably look them up on the online planner we all shared so we knew where we were at nearly all times of the day. It might seem like overreaching to some, but with what we had all been through as a family? No, we needed to know those kinds of things.

I grabbed my bag and could not wait to take off my makeup, get out of my soft silk dress, and into some sweats so I could enjoy myself. I might be a girly-girl, but my mother's idea of lunch attire wasn't my favorite thing.

I walked into the house and frowned at the sound of someone banging a hammer.

It could be Mackenzie—she was the handiest among us, but we weren't that great at household things. We tried, but Mackenzie was the only one who could bang a hammer with that much force. Whatever they were doing, that much power was not for simply hanging a photo.

We all could do that much.

I frowned, suddenly worried that I was home alone with someone violent. I looked around for a weapon and picked up a rolling pin. It would have to do.

I held it tightly, my pulse racing as I slowly walked upstairs. I froze and swallowed hard as I realized that the banging sound was coming from my bedroom.

I probably should have called the cops or at least called out. Done *anything* but what I was doing. However, it had been a long day, and I wasn't thinking clearly.

I slowly made my way to the door and peeked around the edge.

The scream that erupted from my mouth really shouldn't have been a surprise.

Tanner whipped around, pulling out his headphones, and gripped the hammer tightly. Sweat poured down his naked torso, and I did my best not to look down, but I couldn't help it. I had seen him stripping before, and he hadn't been wearing a shirt then. I had run before he had taken off everything else, and I tried not to feel the anger I did over the fact that my friends had seen him strip while I had run away like a little girl.

"What the fuck, Natalie?" he growled. "You just run around with a rolling pin? What were you going to do with that?"

"I thought you were an ax murderer or something," I blurted. I knew right then and there that I would likely never say the right thing when it came to Tanner. I didn't know why, but I lost all sense when it came to him, and I hated myself a little bit more each time I spoke.

He looked at the rolling pin, then at me, and growled.

I snarled right back.

"Are you fucking kidding me right now? You thought I was a murderer? And you were going to come at me with a rolling pin? No, you call *me*. You call the cops. You call anyone. You don't get your pretty little ass up here to fight whoever it is off with a fucking rolling pin."

"I didn't think you were a murderer. I just wondered what was going on upstairs. In my *bedroom*."

"Then you call me, Natalie."

"Why would I call you?" I asked and immediately knew it was probably the wrong thing to say.

His jaw tightened. "Fine, call Dillon. Call anyone else. Just don't come around here and think you can fight off an intruder with a rolling pin. Jesus Christ, Natalie."

"Don't *Jesus Christ* me."

"You don't like me cursing?"

"It's not that, dumbass," I cursed right back. "Stop yelling at me. I was trying to take care of myself."

"So, you picked up a rolling pin? That's what you learned in the self-defense classes you took?"

After Elise had been attacked, we had all taken self-defense classes. I still took them. I was doing better, and I wanted to kick myself because, yes, I had pepper spray and should've used that. But, no, I was an idiot.

I groaned. "I'm so stupid. Please, don't yell at me anymore. Even though I still don't know why you're here. Why are you here?"

"I'm fixing your window," he snapped.

"With no one home? You just let yourself in?" I asked and set down the rolling pin. I was an idiot. I was that stupid heroine in every horror show who got killed at the beginning before the opening credits even rolled. I was Drew Barrymore popping popcorn and talking about scary movies.

"We all have keys. Of course, I let myself in. I can't work around your timeline to fix your house."

"You don't have to fix anything." I sighed.

"Like your landlord's going to do it?"

"He's a dick, but he sometimes sends people."

"Who fuck shit up that I need to fix again anyway."

"Stop being so growly."

"I'm not growly. I'm me. Get over it."

He was right about that. He was just being himself —an asshole.

"Why are you here, Tanner?" I asked, frowning at him. While he was growling at me, he didn't meet my eyes. And that was weird, considering Tanner always met my gaze. It was hard to think around him because that's what he did. He looked straight at me, and it made me swallow hard and think about things I probably shouldn't. He always met everybody's gaze when he talked to them, and he didn't lie. He might not say everything and could lie by omission, but he didn't outright lie. I'd always respected him for that.

"As I said, I'm here to fix your window."

"And?"

"Natalie."

I narrowed my eyes and let out a huff of breath. "You want to make sure I'm not going to tell anybody. I'm not, Tanner. I told you I wouldn't. Have I ever once broken my word to you?"

"No, but you never know. It could happen."

"Really? After all this time, I'm just going to suddenly out you? I would never do that to you, Tanner. I don't know why you're doing what you are. I don't know why that's your chosen profession, but more power to you."

He snorted. "That's what you're going with?"

"What? You're doing it to pay for college, am I right? Good for you."

"I've become a cliché," he said, shaking his head before running his hand through his hair.

"Not really. If I were stripping to pay for college, then *I'd* be a cliché."

He quickly looked over my shoulder, and I sighed. "Nobody's here. They're not going to find out. I'm not going to tell them. Though I don't think they would ever look down on you if you *did* tell them."

"I'm already the poor kid in the group. I don't need to be the poor stripper."

I shook my head. "We don't put labels on each other. And remember, Nessa's the one who might need to drop out of school."

He winced. "Oh."

"So, you see? You're not the saddest case between all of us. If anything, I'm the sad one."

He looked at me and then threw his head back, laughing. "I'm so sorry, little trust fund baby. Tell me how bad your life is."

"I'm not saying it's bad. I was just saying that not everything in life is perfect."

"Why? Didn't get the Prada handbag you wanted?"

"Of course, not. I was looking for Chanel."

His eyes crossed. "I have no idea what any of that means."

"You don't have to. If I wanted to live up to my family's and former friends' expectations, I'd have a Birkin bag. But that's sort of what you get when you get caught up in those circles."

"Seriously, you're saying words, opening your mouth and speaking, yet…nothing."

I shook my head and laughed. "I'm pretty much just rambling at this point."

"Good. While I joke that you're some trust fund baby, you're not like the girls you were with at the club."

I cringed. "I think that's a compliment."

He shrugged as he put his tools away. I did my best not to stare at his muscles. It was challenging not to look.

"I guess it is. They were rude to the staff, at least a few of them were. A couple of them were nice, but they didn't tip well. You left, so I didn't get to see how you tip."

"I would've tipped decently. At least, I think so. I did tip that one waiter."

"Ah, yes, I saw you tip Jason on his way to the other table. Friends of yours?"

I nodded. "Yes. At least friendly acquaintances who could become friends. You know how school is."

"I do," he said as he stuck his hands into his pockets. He still hadn't put on a shirt.

"Who are you, Natalie Blake?" he asked, and I blinked.

"You know who I am, Tanner Hagen."

His eyes lit up. "Do I?"

"You do. You've known me for a couple of years now. I don't keep secrets, Tanner. It's kind of difficult when you have a group of friends who are friendly with another group and we become a conglomerate."

He grinned at me. "I guess that is true."

I had moved into the bedroom, so I was only two feet away from him now, and it was hard to focus. He was just so beautiful. He probably wouldn't have appreciated me thinking that, but he was. His body looked as if it had been chiseled from stone. The angles on his face were harsh, yet his lips were soft. And the way he looked at me? His eyes weren't hard chips of ice. Instead, I saw softness there.

I didn't understand why, though.

"That's a nice dress, Natalie," he said out of the blue.

I blushed. "Thank you. I had lunch with my parents, and my mother picked it out for me to wear."

"You let your mother dress you?"

I crossed my eyes. "No, but this is what she likes, so

why start a fight over something that is easily remedied?"

"You fight with your parents, then?"

I shrugged. "Only about my future. But they're not that bad."

"Hmm," he said.

Why was it so hard to concentrate when he was around? "Anyway, thanks for fixing the window."

"I only somewhat fixed it. I don't have the right tools to finish."

"What tool do you need?" I asked. Given the way he smirked, I couldn't help but wonder exactly where his mind had gone. Of course, when my gaze moved down that chest of his to where that trail of hair disappeared into his jeans, I knew my mind had gone there, too.

"You surprise me so much, Natalie," he whispered. He was so close to me now. I hadn't realized he had moved. Or maybe I had been the one who moved.

I could feel the heat of him. And then his hand was on my face, his palm cupping my cheek, his fingers in my hair.

"What are you doing?" I whispered, my pulse racing.

"Finishing what we started."

And then his lips were on mine, and I groaned. I sighed, wrapping my arms around him. He was hot and slick, and the feel of his naked skin under my palms made me want to swoon right there. Seriously, my knees were about to give out. Tanner had his hand around the back of my neck now, the other on my hip, keeping me steady. His tongue was tentative at first, as if he wondered if I would push him away.

I didn't want to push him away.

We were alone in the house. I wanted him. Why couldn't we do this? Why couldn't this be just for now? It didn't have to be forever.

I didn't need forever.

I arched my back, rubbing my breasts against his chest, and he growled deep in his throat before deepening the kiss.

I shivered at his touch, letting him control things. I didn't mind. I didn't know what I was doing, but I trusted him.

I had faith in him in a way that maybe I shouldn't, but it didn't matter.

He slid his hand down my side to brush his fingertips along the hem of my dress, on the skin of my thighs. I sucked in a breath, and he bit my lip, his gaze piercing.

"Yes?" he asked.

"Yes," I whispered, my voice breathy. Tanner kissed me again, his lips trailing over my cheek, my jaw, down my neck. He had me pressed against the desk, my hands gripping the edge as he slowly moved between my legs.

"Good?" he asked again, and I nodded, pressing closer to him, needing his taste.

He looked at the desk behind me and scowled. "Not sturdy enough for what I want," he snarled, and I nearly came right there.

I might never have had sex with someone, but I knew how to give myself an orgasm. I had done it more than once, probably more than once this week, so I knew exactly how to get myself off.

I just didn't know how to get *him* off.

Tanner moved me towards the bed, the back of my legs hitting the edge, shocking me. I must've let out a little gasp because he grinned before kissing me again. And then I was sitting on the edge of the mattress, my skirt up on my thighs.

He kissed me again, and I clung to him, my fingernails raking down his back. He hummed before dropping to his knees. My eyes widened.

He lifted a single brow, looking like the Devil tempting Eve, and I was ready.

His fingertips slowly ran up my thighs, and I shivered, spreading my legs ever so slightly.

"Naughty little Natalie wants my touch?" he asked.

"Yes," I gasped, not caring that I was needy. I

wanted this. It was what I needed. If Tanner wanted to give, I would take—and give back whatever I could.

If I let myself think too hard, I would run away. We had only shared a few kisses, and we fought more often than not, but here I was, about to let Tanner touch me in ways no other person ever had.

I didn't care at that moment, though. And I hadn't cared when I dreamed about it before. When I imagined this happening. When I had my hand between my legs, orgasming with his name on my lips.

This was a dream made reality—and just for this moment.

Tanner looked at me then and wrapped his hands around the sides of my panties before pulling them down.

I knew I was blushing, awkwardness taking its toll, but he was so sweet. So gentle.

While the others in the house might know of my virginity, I didn't think Tanner did. And I wasn't about to tell him. This wasn't his virginity we were talking about. It was mine.

My right to own, and my right to give.

When I looked down at him, his head between my legs, I knew right then and there that this was what I wanted.

"So pretty and pink," he whispered, and I blushed

a deep red. "Already wet for me." He tugged my dress to my stomach.

I groaned and knew that I would remember this moment until the end of my days.

His fingers moved over my folds, and I jumped. He shook his head before leaning down to blow cool air over me. I shuddered, my head rolling back.

"Let me take care of you, princess," he whispered.

He spread me slightly before his thumb circled my clit. My hips shot off the bed.

"So sensitive," he murmured before leaning in to lick me. I swore I saw stars as I fell back onto the bed, spreading my legs even more. He chuckled roughly against me, but then I couldn't hear him anymore because of the buzzing in my head as he lapped at me, tasting and licking my pussy until I had one leg over his shoulder, the other pinned to the bed as he ate me out.

I came in a rush, my entire body shaking as he growled into me.

When I could finally open my eyes, he stood above me, licking his very wet lips. He wiped his chin, and I knew I should be embarrassed. That was *me* all over his face, but I didn't care.

Because Tanner had just gone down on me and had given me the best orgasm of my life.

My entire body felt warmed from the inside out. My nipples ached, and my toes had gone numb.

From an orgasm. Something I had thought I had given myself multiple times.

Apparently, a Tanner-made orgasm was completely different than a self-made one.

Damn this man. I had known he would be an addiction. Only I hadn't realized I'd succumb so quickly.

"I want to see those pretty breasts," he whispered as he leaned over and undid the tie at my waist.

It was a wrap dress, perfect for this type of moment —as if I had known when I'd put it on that morning.

He pulled the pretty peach silk away before looking down at my lacy bra that barely covered my breasts. I was a big girl up top, had been since puberty, and I had always been a little embarrassed about it. Mostly because my nipples were large, my boobs barely fit into bras that were cute and pretty, and I filled out shirts a little too much for some people.

But given the way Tanner groaned as he cupped them in his hands? I knew that I would now love my breasts until my last day on Earth.

He leaned down and kissed me again. I tasted myself on him. It was sweet, a little tart, and I was already wet for him again. He undid the clasp on my bra. It was the front-clasp type, the only one that kept me up in this dress. When the cups fell to the sides, my breasts followed a bit, the heavy weight of them even more erotic with the movement. My nipples were hard and so sensitive as he brushed them with his tongue, that my hips shot off the bed again and right into him. He groaned and looked up at me.

"Damn, I don't know if I'll be able to last long enough to make you come by just sucking on your breasts. Your nipples are so fucking sensitive. Have you ever come by having some man touch your breasts before?"

I shook my head. "No."

"Good."

Then he sucked on my breasts as promised, one hand going down my stomach before spearing me with two fingers. I shook, nearly coming again before he stopped, leaving me on the precipice. "You're fucking tight, Natalie."

I looked up at him then. "Then you'd better get in me," I panted, more brazen than I had ever been in my life.

He grinned and kissed me hard on the mouth. "You got a condom, princess? Because I don't have one in my wallet."

I bit my lip. "We have a whole drawer of them in the common bathroom. Lots of boyfriends around here."

His gaze met mine, and he nodded slowly before

kissing me again. He left me lying there for a moment, sated and yet on edge all at the same time.

But he was back in an instant, a foil packet in hand. "You sure?"

"Please, Tanner," I nearly begged. "Stop asking. We already went over this."

"Whatever you say, princess." Then he undid his jeans and pulled them down over his hips.

I was pretty sure I swallowed my tongue, and that buzzing sound came again.

Tanner Hagen was hard, thick, and much bigger than I'd thought. I had seen a penis before—at least online. And I thought I knew what an average penis looked like.

Tanner was not average. Oh, no. No, no. He was well above average.

And, once again, I hated that my high school friends had seen that package stuffed into tiny briefs or whatever the hell he'd worn while stripping.

I hated myself a little bit again that I had missed it. But I wasn't missing it now.

He gripped the base of his cock and pumped once, twice.

"You look so wide-eyed. You're giving me the best compliment."

"You don't need a bigger head, do you?" I asked and then blinked before we both burst out laughing.

"Well, then. I don't usually laugh during sex. I kind of like it."

Then he was over me again, kissing me hard. His hands were on my breasts, between my legs, bringing me nearly to orgasm again before placing himself at my entrance and looking down at me. "Ready?" he asked. I swallowed hard and nodded.

"Yes."

He tangled his fingers of one hand with mine and used the other to guide himself into me. He was big, far too big, but it didn't matter. I stretched, I burned, and everything hurt for a second. I moaned, and he worked my clit with his fingers as he kissed me hard again, easing his way slowly in and out of me. An inch in, and then back again. He slowly repeated the process until he was seated deep inside of me, and both of us were shaking and sweat-slick. I couldn't breathe.

"So fucking tight, princess. I'm going to come right now."

"Move," I whispered, feeling so full I couldn't even think. Everything hurt, and yet I was right on the edge of something blissful. I knew it. If he just moved, everything would make sense, and I would be able to breathe again. I would be able to do something.

Tanner pulled back slightly, and I groaned, gripping him.

He met my gaze, something passing over his eyes that I couldn't read, and then he moved.

It took me a moment to find a rhythm, to figure out what I was supposed to do, but I moved with him, needing him, arching for him.

He was so gentle, so sweet. Until he wasn't. And then he pounded into me. But it didn't hurt anymore. I was so close, so needy. When I finally came, he groaned my name into my ear, not *princess*, and shuddered above me. Then he rolled to his side as both of us came down.

It wasn't until he brushed my cheek with his thumb, his gaze piercing mine, that I realized I was crying.

His eyes went blank, and he snarled. "What the hell, Natalie? Don't tell me you were a fucking virgin."

Four

Tanner

The silence was deafening. I looked down at Natalie, and guilt, shame, and rage warred within me.

She frowned, and I cursed under my breath before sliding out of her, hating that just the friction against my dick made me hard again.

I got up, took care of the condom, and let out a breath.

She had to have been a virgin. In the back of my mind, I had known that, hadn't I? Hadn't I heard her talking with the others about it? Or maybe it had been

Corinne, the friend we had lost last year. I couldn't remember. Still, it felt as if it were coming to the forefront now.

I was such a fucking idiot.

I'd just had sex with a virgin. Hard sex. And, yes, I'd made her come, but I hadn't been gentle. Someone's first moment should be memorable and sweet.

It didn't need to be a hard fuck in the afternoon with a somewhat friend. Someone with which there could be no future.

I quickly looked under her sink for a hand towel, picked one, ran it under some warm water, and went out to the bedroom. She sat at the edge of the bed, working to put her bra back on. I couldn't help but look at her beauty. Her long, blond hair floated around her, the waves natural, but I knew she also used a heating tool of some sort in the mornings. She looked a little ragged around the edges, and that was all on me. She had been sweet and contained when she showed up earlier, and I had ruined all of that.

It seemed I was good at ruining a lot of fucking things these days.

Natalie was all curves set in a compact frame. She was gorgeous, sinful, and yet innocent. Although not quite so innocent anymore since I had ruined that.

Anger filled me, but not at her. Never at her.

I stomped over to her. She looked up at me, her throat working as she swallowed hard.

I was still naked, my cock hardening again at just the sight of her, and I didn't care.

"Let me help clean you up," I growled. She frowned at me. "Of course, you wouldn't know what happens next."

"Stop getting angry with me," she ordered. "I know what I'm supposed to do. I have friends."

She snatched the towel from me, and I grabbed it right back. "At least let me take care of you, goddamn it."

My gaze was on hers as I slid the towel between her legs. It was an intimate gesture. Something I wasn't prepared for. Her mouth parted. "Feel okay?" I whispered.

"I…thank you." Her voice was soft, and I hated myself again.

I swallowed hard, backed up, and then bent to pick up my jeans. She grabbed her dress and scurried to the bathroom, closing the door behind her. I knew I should leave. Just go so we didn't have to talk about it. However, that was the coward's way out. And while I was many things, I wasn't a coward.

At least, I hoped I wasn't.

I pulled my shirt back on and sat on her desk chair to slide my feet into my boots. She returned, this time in cute sweats and a T-shirt, though I had to wonder where she'd gotten the clothes.

She noticed my frown, and a blush crept over those cheeks of hers.

"I had a pile of clothes in there. I have some work to do, and I would rather be comfortable than in that dress."

"Ah."

"Since you asked, yes, I was a virgin. I've had sex with myself before, of course. I've had orgasms and even used toys, so you weren't the first penetration I've ever had."

My eyes widened at the clinical nature of her words, but as I looked up at her face, her chin rose, and I saw the nervousness there.

"Good to know, but you still should have told me."

"Why?"

"Because I was your first. Now I'm the fucking asshole who took your virginity without even knowing. I fucked you hard into a bed, Natalie. It shouldn't have been me."

She narrowed her eyes and let out a slight snarl. It was damn cute, and I did my best to ignore it. "Virginity and virtue are a construct created by man to subjugate women."

I blinked. "That's what you're going with?"

"That's exactly what I'm going with. Yes, you were

the first person I had sex with. Other than myself. I guess I could say *I* took my virginity depending on how you want to think about it."

Hell, it was going to be so fucking hard not to fall in love with her. When Hagens fell, they fell hard and fast. But I couldn't let it be her. I wasn't good for her. "Stop getting into fucking semantics."

"I don't know what you want from me. In this case, virginity is all about semantics."

I wanted a whole hell of a lot, but I didn't say that. "Why me?"

"Why *not* you, Tanner?"

"I'm a jerk to you. We're barely friends."

She flinched. "Thanks."

Fucking asshole. "You know what I mean. Whenever we're together, we're usually yelling at each other or snarling."

"Or helping each other with papers, or you're doing housework for me while I cook for you. We are friends, Tanner."

"Why did you wait so damn long if you were only going to have sex with me some random afternoon? I thought you would want it to be special."

She blushed again. "It was special. It's something that I chose. I didn't have sex before because I didn't have a boyfriend I *wanted* to have sex with. Or a girlfriend, for that matter. It just didn't come up—and don't make a dirty joke," she added quickly.

I snorted. "Fine, I still don't know why me."

"I like you. And not like that, Tanner, so you can just get that panic out of your eyes. I like you. I respect you. So, yes, we had sex. Now, we don't have to talk about it anymore. Especially if you're going to act like this." She folded her arms under her breasts, and I did my best to maintain eye contact. It was tough when all I wanted to do was put my mouth on those nipples of hers again. They were so fucking perfect, and I loved how they hardened in my mouth, becoming little points like red cherries.

Fuck, I needed to stop thinking about her like that.

"Damn it, Natalie. I don't know what we're supposed to do now."

She bit her lip, and I wanted to lean down and brush my tongue over it. This was going to be a problem. Yet I knew it had been an issue long before this. Hence why I did my best to stay away from her.

"We don't have to do anything about it. It was a moment, and now we can walk away as friends and keep doing what we've been doing."

We both knew that wouldn't happen, but I wasn't sure I could say that.

"You're okay? I didn't hurt you?" And that was the crux of the problem. I'd had sex before, lots of it. I'd been in a poly relationship for nearly a year before this. I liked sex and thought I was damn good at it, but I'd never been with a virgin before. I'd never been with Natalie before. Why did it feel like everything was already different?

She smiled softly, and my dick got hard again. "I'm fine. It was great, Tanner. I'm not going to say it was nice because that would be disrespectful to both of us, but I had fun. I promise. And we can just talk like we used to—and not talk about this again."

She was giving me an easy out, and I hated that I wanted to take it.

My phone buzzed, and I looked down at the alarm. "Fuck. I have to go into work." Her eyes widened, and I snorted. "Hey, at least I don't have to lie to you about where I'm going anymore."

"As long as you enjoy what you're doing," she muttered.

Was that jealousy in her tone? I didn't think so. I was a little too confused after the day, and I didn't know what we were doing.

"It pays the bills. I won't have to keep doing it for long. And I don't get fully naked, so there's that."

"I'm kind of glad you don't, although maybe that is the selfish part of me talking." She winked as she said it. I swallowed hard. I knew I could just leave, but I didn't. I moved forward, cupped her face, and lowered my lips to hers. She was so soft against me and let out a breath as I kissed her.

"Be safe," I whispered. Then, I hugged her hard like I always did because I loved how she felt against me, all soft yet not mine. "I've got to go, Natalie."

"Just don't say you're sorry," she mumbled against me. I felt as if I'd been kicked in the gut. I had almost said those words, but if I had, she never would have forgiven me. So, instead, I kissed the top of her head, ran my hand down her back, and left.

I did need to go to work. Natalie knew that. Still, I was the asshole who'd left the girl whose virginity he'd just taken all alone in her room.

I was going to a very special hell.

I rolled my shoulders back and headed out of the house. Thankfully, nobody had come home in the time I'd been there because we had left Natalie's door open, and anyone would have been able to see and hear what we had done. I hadn't told Natalie not to tell her friends. If she told the girls what had happened, then so be it. I would deal with the consequences as long as Natalie didn't need to deal with them. If they looked down on her for sleeping with me? Then I'd have to say something. I didn't mind what they thought about me, but fuck if they'd make Natalie feel bad for enjoying herself.

I made my way down to the club, parked in the

employee lot, and walked through the back door. I nodded at a few bouncers getting ready and setting up, and at the bartender also prepping for the evening. I made my way back to the locker room and was grateful to see that I was one of the first people there, so I didn't have to deal with any questioning glances. I liked most of the people I worked with, just not everybody. Some were assholes, and some wanted more from one another than just stripping. That wasn't me. I was here to do a job. To get in and get out. I didn't do some of the back-room things that some of the other dancers did. Not that they did anything on the grounds, but there *were* other ways to make money, and the boss turned a blind eye as long as those things weren't done in the club itself.

I saw JC sitting on the bench, looking in his locker for something, and went over to the older man—my one good friend here.

"What's troubling you, Tanner?" JC asked, his deep baritone vibrating in a grumble.

I lifted my chin. "You haven't even looked up at me. How the hell do you know anything's wrong?"

"You're stomping your feet as you walk," he answered as he pulled out his leather pants with the hidden snaps on the side.

"Well, fuck," I said, looking down at my boots. "That's good to know."

"Can't change your tread, even though I know you would try, just to spite me."

"Thanks," I said dryly.

"So, what's wrong?" he asked as he looked towards me, his brown eyes piercing. JC was about six-five, all muscle and dark brown skin that shone under the fluorescent lighting.

He raised a brow at me, and I sighed.

"A lot is going on, And I know that I only have another few months before I'm done with this."

"Good for you," he said dryly.

I winced. "Not that working here is wrong," I corrected.

JC snorted. "Yeah, no. We're not going to go into that," the other man said. "I'm working here as a second job. The medical bills will dwindle soon, and I won't need it anymore."

I grinned. "You and Zeke are okay, then?"

JC and Zeke had been together for nearly twenty years, married for the past five. Zeke had gotten sick right before their wedding, and they were still dealing with the debt from medical bills.

"Almost done. Maybe we'll be finished at the same time."

"From your mouth to the bouncers' ears," I mumbled.

"Now, tell me what's going on."

"I slept with Natalie," I blurted, and JC's eyes widened.

For some reason, I could bare my soul to JC. He knew all about me losing my dad in Afghanistan and me having to support my mother and little brother. He knew about the asshole who wanted to be my stepdad, and about the roommates and all of the women. He knew about my exes, the poly relationship I had been in that had formed into a cheating nightmare, even though I was still friends with them.

JC knew nearly everything about me, and he told me a lot about his life, as well, even though we didn't hang out much except for at the café after we were both done with work. He was like my sponsor, but maybe for an addiction to fucking things up rather than drinking.

"Well, then. It looks like we're going to have a fun conversation after work tonight."

I cringed. "It just happened. Literally right before I came here."

"That's why you look somewhat sated and strung out all at once? Good to know. Put it into your act tonight. Make a few extra bucks. And then we'll talk about it."

"I shouldn't have touched her, JC."

"Why do you think that?" he asked as he shucked his jeans. I did the same, getting ready for my shift.

"I'm not good enough for her. We both know it."

"You're lucky we're on work grounds, or I'd slap you upside the head."

"It wouldn't help. Nothing's going to pry what's up there loose."

"You're an idiot."

"I'm not. Natalie is on such a different level."

"Levels can be even. One doesn't need to be better than the other."

"The whole point of levels is that you go up or down."

"Unless they're in two separate buildings, and you're both on the same wavelength."

"I have no idea what this metaphor even means anymore," I grumbled, and JC laughed.

"She's not better than you because she comes from money. She's not better than you because of her degree. She's not better than you because she doesn't work here. She's just different. And something must have happened to allow you to sleep with each other. That's something you'll need to think on. Something we'll talk about later."

He gestured over his shoulder, and I looked as a few other people walked in, all laughing and getting ready for the evening.

I sighed and started putting on my uniform.

Tonight, I would be the bad boy on stage, using what fate had given me so I could pay for school.

I gyrated, rolled my hips, and brooded at the crowd. All for money so I could have a life.

While Natalie sat at home, working on her homework and getting ready to be a social worker. She would save the world while I was merely living in it.

I shouldn't have touched her. Even before I knew she was a virgin, she had been off-limits.

And I had taken something that didn't belong to me. While the selfish part of me wanted more, everything else knew I shouldn't.

I knew it was a mistake.

I couldn't touch her again, no matter how much I wanted to. No matter how much I'd *always* wanted to.

FIVE

Natalie

Did I look different? No. Maybe a little more confused, peaceful, or even energized in the eyes if I looked closely. But that wasn't the case in truth.

Not when I honestly thought about it.

I was no longer a virgin.

Ring the bell, sound the alarm, tell the town crier.

Natalie Blake had lost that pesky virginity.

I knew I should probably feel different than I did, and yet I wasn't even sure *what* I felt. It'd happened perfectly. While Tanner might not think so, I did. It was what I'd wanted. When I wanted it. And with the person I wanted it with. Tanner might not be my forever, but he had been my right then, and that was all that mattered. I still didn't think I had owed him an explanation beforehand. Yet I felt terrible about it. I didn't feel bad that he had been the one I'd slept with, but that he felt responsible for that fact. It wasn't like I could apologize to him, though. That would just be ridiculous.

Our afternoon had been nearly three days ago now, and we hadn't spoken since. That wasn't too different than usual. We were all in the middle of school and dealing with our lives. I had internship hours, volunteer hours, and charity work on top of my classes. I didn't know when I slept, but I made things work. When I saw Tanner next, I wasn't sure how I was supposed to act or how I would react, yet in the end, all that mattered was that we remained friends. At least, that's what I told myself.

Tonight, however, was not about that. No, it was all about dinner with the family again. I didn't usually have so many meals with them, but I knew my mother was trying to make sure I was happy. And if that meant getting married, even better. That was her goal.

Which was why I currently sat at my family's formal dining room table, wearing a fancy dress and pearl earrings as I sat next to an older gentleman who was, apparently, my date.

He was some friend of my father's, though not as old as my dad. In his late thirties or early forties, he was kind, a widower, and seemed to be looking for wife number two.

He was a great man, and I vaguely remembered meeting him when I was younger.

However, he was at least fifteen years older than me, we had nothing in common other than my parents, and he didn't seem to be at all interested in whatever my mother had planned. He'd probably thought he was coming over to schmooze with my father and had ended up on an accidental date with me.

I'm quite the prize, it seems.

I ignored that dark thought and did my best to focus on what was in front of me.

"Natalie is almost finished with her degree. I love that it will help her so much with the charities we run as a family."

I looked up at that as my mother smiled over at Arnold.

I loved my mother. I really did. She wasn't cruel, wasn't too demanding. But this was laying it on a little thick. And she didn't seem to understand that I wouldn't be following in her footsteps.

"I hope that it will help me in my charity work,

but I also plan on going into social work. Children and families need help, and I want to be there. That's why I'm getting my degree. And I'm not done yet. I want a master's, as well." I looked over at Arnold, who smiled softly at me. There was genuine interest in his eyes, at least about my plans. He was friendly and didn't seem too bored with what I was talking about.

That had to count as something. It just wouldn't count for precisely what he was thinking, or at least what my parents were thinking.

My dad looked over at my mother, and I saw the exasperation in his expression.

Dad was usually on board with my mother's schemes to marry me off, but this might've been stretching things a little too far. After all, Dad would have to go golfing with Arnold later. I wondered to myself if Arnold drank Arnold Palmers. I held back a snort that wouldn't be ladylike and ignored my mother's groan. She could always tell when my mind wandered, and it seemed today was no different.

"Are you looking for universities now? I'm trying to remember what the timing is on that."

The subtle comment about the difference in our ages and what he remembered hit home, and he blushed.

He was a nice man, but did nothing for me. All I

could think about was Tanner and how he moved, the way he tasted, and how he'd touched me.

And that was enough of that for tonight.

My mother could practically read my thoughts, and I had a feeling that once she met Tanner, she would know exactly where my mind went far too often.

"I'm working on them now. Deadlines are coming up soon. Then, hopefully, we'll be able to hear back, and I can do school visits. I want to stay in the state, though, since most of our charities are here."

Arnold nodded. "That makes sense. I know of a few good programs in Boulder. And the university you're going to. Would it be wrong for you to stay there?"

I shook my head as I sipped my wine. "No, I could continue, and my advisor for undergrad thinks I'd be a good fit. That would be nice and easy." I winked as I said it, and Arnold smiled. I ignored the clutch in my belly at the pleased look on my mother's face. There wasn't even a single lick of interest in Arnold's eyes when it came to me, but my mother was like a dog with a bone.

I would be stuck with whatever charade she came up with next. As if on cue, she spoke. "Are you sure you need to go for a full master's? I do appreciate how much you're working towards your education, Natalie, but do you need all that for social work?"

I held back a sigh and sipped my wine. "For what I want to do, yes. It will be good for me because I don't feel ready yet to dive headfirst into things. I'm going to need a few more clinical hours, as well. Therefore, I'll need to work as hard as I can to make sure that happens. Between finals coming up and making sure I get to stay in the classes I want for next semester, I'll be busy for the next few weeks." I gave my mom a pointed look, and she raised a brow at me. I ignored her. I loved my mother, though I once again had to remind myself of that fact.

By the time we were through with dinner, dessert, and after-dinner drinks, I was exhausted but kept a polite smile on my face as I said goodbye to Arnold.

My mother and father gave us some privacy, and I knew they weren't listening in—though they were probably hoping for something more. I held back a sigh.

"I hope it's not out of place for me to say this," Arnold began, and I looked up at him.

"Oh?" I asked, a little worried.

"You're a lovely girl—I mean woman..." he corrected, and I held back a snort. "You are kind, and you have a great future ahead of you. But I don't think either of us is quite interested in what your mother might have in mind."

I held back a cringe. "No. I don't want to hurt your

feelings, but I'm not interested in what my mother wants. I'm not sure about my father, so don't think poorly of him when you see him next."

Relief spread over his face, and I smiled.

"Not that you aren't lovely and beautiful and most likely insanely brilliant and talented, but I don't think that dating my friend and colleague's nearly teenage daughter is the right way for me to go to find my next romance."

I grinned. "That was a very nice way of putting that."

"I'm trying. Now, if you'd like, I can make sure that this isn't an issue for you."

"What do you mean?" I asked.

"I can talk to your father and make sure that he knows I'm the one who's not interested if that will be easier for you."

And my appreciation for Arnold grew. Not that I wanted to have anything to do with him, but he was kind.

"You don't have to worry. I'll talk with my parents. I don't want things to be awkward between you guys at work. I know you and my dad are friends. I'm always awkward with my parents. It's what we do. Sadly, you're not the first random date who's been at a family dinner that didn't go as planned," I added dryly.

"I'm sorry about that. You seem a little busy."

I finally cringed and looked down at my watch. "So busy, in fact, that I am now late to meet my roommates."

"I would say I'll see you soon, but let's make it a little bit longer," he added, winking.

I laughed and rose on tiptoe to kiss his cheek like a good friend. "Thank you," I whispered.

"You've got it, Natalie. Have a good night."

He walked away, and I turned to see my mother glaring at me.

"What?" I asked.

"The kiss on the cheek was a nice touch, but I know you just pushed him away."

I sighed and picked up my bag. "We pushed each other away, Mother. Arnold, really? He seems like a great guy, but he's nearly your and Dad's age."

"She's got you there, darling," Dad said from the doorway. "Drive home safely. Text us when you get there."

"I will."

"You can't stay for longer?" Mother asked, frowning. She would have preferred I still live with them. And while I understood that, I needed to get out from under their thumbs. They wanted me safe, I knew that, but I needed space.

"I will see you guys later. Two dinners within a

week have eaten into my homework time. Not that I don't love you."

I kissed them both and headed out, ignoring my mother saying that she would do better with the next try.

I knew that tonight was just another in the string of random dates my mother set me up on. Maybe if I were dating someone, it wouldn't be like this. But the only person I wanted to date was the one I couldn't have. I would deal with my mother and what she wanted for now.

Maybe she would see me as the adult I was someday and let me make the choices I needed to make for my life on my own.

I drove home, tired but knowing I needed to stay up for a few more hours. It was Friday night, and my roommates were going out later tonight with their boyfriends to a club. Not Tanner's club, though. Which was good. From what I could tell, he was working tonight—not that he told anyone else that.

I planned to stay home, try to get some homework done, and then go to bed with a headache and probably a backache from leaning over applications for too long.

I pulled into the driveway and moved off to the side so the girls could get in and out when they needed.

I wasn't sure who was driving tonight—or if they were at all.

I walked inside and sighed happily at the scent of perfume, the sound of laughter, and the warmth of good friends.

I missed Corinne more than I could say. She had been our friend and had died of a brain aneurysm over a year ago now. Elise had walked into the house to find Corinne lying on the floor, shattering our lives. We actually moved out of that nice place into this crappier house because of it. And while I understood why we had to leave—the idea of walking back into that house being too much for any of us—I still missed that place often. I wasn't a huge fan of the home we lived in now, but I tried not to be too pretentious about it.

The landlord was a jerk and never fixed anything we asked him to, hence why Tanner came over often to help. Like with the window. And another time when he had fixed the lock on the door.

He was keeping us safe, like all the guys were, yet I wasn't sure what I was supposed to think about it.

"You're here. We thought you'd be home earlier." Nessa smiled as she handed me a glass of wine. "Want a taste?"

I looked at it and figured…why the hell not? I'd only had a sip of mine at dinner, and I could work over textbooks with a second glass of wine in my system. Hopefully.

"Are you sure you don't want to go out with us?" Elise asked as she looked in the mirror, fixing her lipstick.

The girls looked amazing, each in short dresses, high heels, their hair done to perfection.

They looked gorgeous and were now going out for the evening with their boyfriends while I was just coming home from a family dinner, about to get into my PJs to do some homework.

There was something wrong with that scenario.

"The unexpected dinner tonight cut into my homework time. So, while you guys probably finished yours, I now need to begin."

"Damn families getting in the way." Elise rolled her eyes and hugged me tightly. "If you change your mind, you already look gorgeous. Come on out."

I looked down at my conservative, neutral tan dress and snorted. "Yes, I'll fit right in out there clubbing with y'all."

"We try," Mackenzie said as she pushed her hair away from her face. "Pacey just texted. They're sitting outside. There's nowhere to park on the street since there appears to be a couple of parties across the way. Oh, and somebody blocked you in, Natalie."

I scowled. "I even parked off to the side so it would be easy for you guys to get out."

"That's what Pacey said." Mackenzie held up her phone. "Anyway, we need to rush out since they're double-parked, and some jackass is honking at them. We love you." They all hugged and kissed me and then left. I shook my head and locked the door behind them.

I didn't deadbolt it since I knew they would be coming back tonight—at least, I figured. I wasn't positive. They could stay at the guys' place. So, I shot them a quick text to make sure.

Elise texted back that they were all sleeping at the guys' house tonight unless I wanted one of them to come back.

Feeling like the seventh wheel, I told them that I didn't need them, that I was fine being alone, and deadbolted the door.

"It's just you and me," I said to the wineglass and wondered briefly if I should get in a cuter dress and make my way out to the club with the girls. Or maybe even go see Tanner.

No, that wasn't in the cards. I would not go back to that strip club. Not that seeing Tanner strip wouldn't be amazing, but it'd be far too tempting.

I went into the kitchen, stuck my wine glass in the fridge, and got my bottle of water. I needed to focus on schoolwork to have the next afternoon off. I could indulge later.

I had just closed the fridge when a circuit popped, and the power went out.

"Fuck," I muttered, grateful that I had my phone in my hand. It was dark outside and seemed even darker in the house. I turned on the flashlight app on my phone, set down my water, and walked towards the laundry room where the breakers were.

The landlord needed to fix this because the power kept going out at odd times, scaring the crap out of me. He knew it, and we knew it, but nothing had been done yet. Something was wrong with the wiring or something. But, apparently, it wasn't that bad, at least according to an electrician the landlord had sent out.

I wasn't sure if I believed that, but I didn't know if a landlord could have electricians under his thumb. This wasn't a mob movie.

I reset the breaker and sighed with relief when everything came back on.

"See? I can do things on my own. I don't need to call Tanner every time something breaks."

At least, that's what I told myself.

Some part of me had wanted to call Tanner immediately, and another part was grateful that I knew he was at work.

Relying on Tanner would be far too easy and much

too dangerous. I would do what I was good at: find my way by myself.

And I would forget that I knew what it felt like to lean on Tanner, even for an evening.

Six

Tanner

"What are we making tonight?" Miles asked as he looked between Dillon and me.

Dillon snorted, and I winked.

"You mean what are Dillon and I making? Because you're not coming anywhere near this stove." I pointed my knife at him.

Miles held up both hands and grinned. "What, I'm doing better. Nessa is teaching Natalie and me how to cook."

My stomach did that little flipping thing at the

mention of Natalie's name, but I ignored it. I could not think about Natalie just then. If I did, it would probably show on my face, and the others would want to know what was wrong.

What *was* wrong?

Everything. Me, mostly.

"We are making chicken pasta Caprese, along with a true Caprese salad and some garlic bread."

"I can help with the garlic bread," Miles put in.

Pacey pulled our roommate back. "How about you help me set the table?"

Miles groaned, and we all laughed. "How am I ever going to learn if you don't let me help?"

"He has us there," Dillon added, and I shrugged.

"Okay fine. You can help cook the pasta."

"The pasta?" Dillon asked, his eyes wide. "Not the pasta. What if he makes it mushy? That's the whole meal."

"How about he cuts the tomatoes?" I asked, and Dillon shook his head. "No, if he bruises them, it'll make *that* mush."

"The mozzarella?"

Dillon shook his head again. "No, same reasoning."

"Can I at least plate the salad once you do all the cutting?" Miles asked, and Dillon gave me a look.

I nodded. "That works."

Miles rolled his eyes. "Thank you so much. I'm so happy."

"You do realize that they're going to be pointing where to put each slice of tomato, basil, and mozzarella, right?" Pacey said dryly, and Miles shrugged.

"It's something, at least."

"We're not that bad, are we?" I winced.

Dillon shrugged. "I think we're worse than that."

"That's good to know," I grumbled. "Now, let's get to cooking and open that bottle of wine. I could use it."

"Tough day?" Dillon asked.

I shrugged. "Normal day, I guess."

"You want to talk about it?"

"Just papers and a project due. Why group projects exist in this day and age, I don't know."

"Probably just to annoy us," Dillon said with a shrug.

"I have to make a plan for a commercial building with three other people. And we have to agree on things. Considering I've been in a poly relationship where communication is key, you would think I would be able to do this. But no, there's no communicating with these people."

"You do realize that once we get out into the real world, we're going to have to work with other people, right? That means tough projects where we get paid but end up doing most of the work because that's who we are."

I cringed at Dillon's words as I began chopping garlic. "That's a nice thought. Thank you for making me feel better."

"I try."

"How's the bar doing? Your family?"

Dillon smiled. "They're doing great. We're busier than ever with the new restaurant opening soon. While part of me wishes I could be at both restaurants and be the chef, that wasn't in the cards. You know?"

"I get it. We're allowed to change our minds a few times."

"Did you?"

I shook my head. "Not really. My dad and I always talked about me becoming an architect, and it sort of just clicked. When I was younger, I thought maybe I would end up joining the military like he did, but then I got a scholarship that paid for most of my first year here, so I ended up staying."

"I'm sorry about your dad," he said after a moment, and I nodded tightly.

"You know how it is to lose people you care about."

"Your dad sounded like a good guy. My parents? Not so much," Dillon replied dryly.

"Maybe, but you've got your brothers and sisters-in-law now."

"True. And my niece."

"I've seen the photos. Are they ever going to come here and visit?" I asked.

"Violet wants to, but Cameron keeps holding her back in case we get overwhelmed by the thought of a child or something."

I rolled my eyes. "Tell them to come over. I want to meet this baby niece of yours."

Dillon grinned. "She is fricking adorable. Somehow, we've become that scene from *Sweet Home Alabama* with a baby in the bar."

I laughed outright. "They've got to start young, at least when it comes to working. Maybe not for the drinking."

"Exactly. Seriously, though, I'll tell them to visit. I know that Elise wants to show off my niece to the girls, and it'd be easier if we were all in one place rather than us trying to find time to make it up to the bar."

"Whatever's easier. But they would probably be more relaxed here."

"Next time we all have time off, I'll make it work. Thanks."

I shrugged. "No problem."

Miles and Pacey came back in, and we worked hard on dinner before moving to the living room to eat. We could have sat in the dining room, but we liked sitting on the big leather couches and relaxing. I ended up on the floor so I didn't spill down my front as I was prone to do, but we were comfortable, all of us talking about school and work and women. Well, *their* women.

"You and Nessa doing okay?" I asked.

Miles shrugged. "I guess so. We'll see."

I didn't like the sound of that, but with the end of the semester approaching, and the two of them constantly circling around one another, I wasn't going to pry. Much. I liked Miles. We were closer than I was with the other two roommates—though Dillon, Pacey, and I had grown together over the past year or so. It was odd since I wasn't usually good at making friends. I was too busy working or dealing with my family to want that. And most of the people I hung out with always found it odd that I came from the town I did, and the circumstances of that.

We used to do better when we had full military pay coming in. It hadn't been great, but it had been enough to get by. Then, when we lost that, the widows' stipend or whatever the hell they called it wasn't enough to do much. Mom worked sixty-hour weeks, and I was often left alone. I worked when I could when I was a teenager. And then when I hit college and found a job at the club, I'd been able to send more money back. Mom still didn't know what I did, and she never would. I didn't want to see the look on her face if she found out that I took off my clothes for money so my kid brother could have food.

I didn't want the shame to creep over either of us.

That just reminded me that Natalie knew, and she hadn't judged.

Why had I thought she would, though? She was a good person, but she also came from a far different family than I did.

Some part of me had just assumed that she wouldn't want to be near anybody who worked in such a low-class establishment. At least, it was low-class to anyone who hadn't been there before. I liked what I did—in the capacity that I was good at it, anyway. And I only felt shitty when I thought about what other people might think.

JC would kick my ass for saying that, though, so I had to be better about it. At least, marginally.

And I needed to stop thinking about Natalie. She wasn't for me. She would never be for me. And the quicker I remembered that, the easier it would be for everybody.

I knew she hadn't told the girls about what had happened. If she had, I'd have probably been punched in the face already. By which guy, I didn't know. But it would happen. They were all dating members within the girls' house, but that wasn't for me. Natalie was sweet and fucking innocent—though I had taken that from her. Yes, she had given that to me, free of any strings, but I still felt those strings wrapping around my neck. They might not be from her, but they were there, ones I wrapped around myself.

"Why are you so serious over there?" Dillon asked, frowning.

I shook my head. "Just thinking about homework," I lied.

"Did it help?" Miles asked, and I grinned.

"No, it's not math or science, but good to know you're there for me."

"I'd be there for the math," Pacey said with a laugh.

"Again, good to know." I sighed. They all started talking about the end of the semester and what we had planned for the holidays. I just sighed. Sadly, the holidays meant I could make decent money at the club. Lonely people who didn't have anyone to spend their holidays with always came in, and I made bank. No more ones. More like twenties and hundreds, as if they were ashamed to be there—or just lonely.

I'd have to deal with more propositions than ever, but that was fine. I was used to it.

Just one more semester after this, and I could get a real job. At least, I hoped. As long as nobody figured out what I did for a living now. One more semester and

I could be a true adult and figure out the rest of my life. Only that life would not include Natalie Blake.

She wasn't for me. I knew that. She had to know that. And the rest of our friends would surely know that if they ever found out what had happened in her room.

As long as I reminded myself that I wasn't good enough for her, maybe I could stop dreaming about her. Stop wanting her.

The next time I saw her, I wouldn't kiss her. Every time I was with her now, I wanted to kiss her, and that was a problem.

One I was afraid I would never be able to fix.

Seven

Natalie

I smiled as the professor droned on and on about my paper and nodded along, doing my best not to throw up. Not that the praise wasn't lovely, because I had worked for days on that paper and was proud of it. No, it had more to do with the fact that I needed to literally throw up. Nausea crept over me, and I swallowed hard, that familiar warmth settling in my throat as I tried to hold back anything unwanted from making an appearance.

I could not believe I was about to throw up on my

professor, but I wasn't going to have a choice soon if he didn't let me out of here.

"Ms. Blake? Are you okay? You've gone rather pale."

I set my hand on my stomach and tried to give him a small smile. Only I couldn't as I was afraid I'd vomit all over him if I opened my mouth.

"Ms. Blake?"

"I'm so sorry," I muttered, letting out a slow breath. "I'm not feeling well." He blinked, seeming to get the message before giving me a quick shake of his head and scrambling back, leaving distance between us as if he were afraid I might vomit on his shoes.

Though that was an option if I weren't careful. I nodded quickly and could have kicked myself for doing so as my stomach roiled.

Making too many rapid movements was probably the wrong move in this case. I nearly ran to the nearest restroom down the hall and was grateful to find it empty.

I set my bag on the hook and dropped to my knees, vomiting up everything I had been able to keep down that morning—mainly just coffee, water, and a few crackers. But this wasn't the first time I had thrown up in the past few days.

Sweat dampened my forehead, but I ignored it as I emptied the rest of my stomach and whatever bile tended to stay back. I used a tissue to clean up, flushed the toilet, and made my way to the sink. I washed my hands thoroughly, rinsed out my mouth, and splashed water on my face.

It wasn't the dirtiest bathroom I'd ever been in in my life, but it wasn't the greatest, either.

I just wanted to go home and shower, but I didn't think I even had the energy to complete that task.

I leaned against the mirror slightly and tried to catch my breath. I had one more class for the day, but I knew I wouldn't make it through. I needed to go home, rest, and just breathe.

I'd been sick off and on for the past couple of weeks, but I hadn't run a fever. I knew I needed to go in and see my doctor. Maybe it was just stress. Between school, my charity work, and volunteering, I didn't have much time to relax.

The times I did, I was with friends, enjoying their happiness and love lives while sitting next to Tanner and pretending that I hadn't slept with him. Making believe that we weren't well aware of what we looked like naked.

No, we hadn't talked about it again. We pretended that it had never happened. Maybe that was for the best, as I wasn't sure I could handle any more stress.

I sighed and made my way to my car, smiling at a few people as I did. I was always seeing people I knew from school, charity work, or my mother's friends. They seemed to be everywhere I looked these days. Or maybe I just happened to know many people. I sighed and got into my car, then headed home.

At the stop sign, I did my best not to vomit again, knowing I really needed to get home.

The sooner I got there, the sooner I could get out of these clothes, shower, and pretend that everything was okay.

Something caught my eye, and I looked to the right to see a woman pushing a stroller, one hand on her swollen belly. The little girl of about two kicked her legs and grinned, and the mom looked so happy, though she did look almost ready to burst.

I blinked before I froze.

I did some quick mental math and swallowed hard.

"Oh, no. No, no, no. That can't be right."

I did the math again and nearly threw up once more.

The car behind me honked, and I looked up, noticing that the light was green. I winced and made my way forward, hitting the gas a little too hard. My tires squealed, and the mother held her stomach tighter, glaring at me.

I sighed and made my way to the next lights before turning. I couldn't go home now. I had to think. If I went home, the others would know. They'd be able to read my thoughts.

Not that they knew what had happened between Tanner and me, but still. This couldn't be happening.

I was not late. Right? No, I'd had my period a few weeks ago. No, that wasn't right, either. A *few weeks ago* was now more than four.

And I was regular. Which meant, something was wrong.

Maybe it's just stress, I told myself again. Yet, as fear crept over my body, I kept driving. I drove away from my neighborhood, away from where my parents' neighborhood cut off, and away from anyone who might know me.

I wasn't even sure if this was the right direction, but if I headed west, I knew there would be mountains there, and I wouldn't end up hitting anything. I'd have to stop sometime.

I finally pulled over into a grocery store, one I'd never been to before, but it looked the same as the grocery store I went to often.

My knees shook as I made my way through and picked up a basket.

I wasn't even focusing as I put a random array of products in the little handcart. Anything that looked good, something that wouldn't stand out against what I needed to pick up. A loaf of bread. Some sandwich meat. A little round of cupcakes. Those looked cute, right?

I nearly wanted to throw up again, but I didn't know if it was the sight of the food or what I was really here for.

I stood in the aisle, shaking, knowing I couldn't do this alone.

I pulled out my phone and wanted to cry.

Me: *We need to talk.*

I slid it back into my bag, knowing I'd hear it chime if he texted back. Then I picked up the pregnancy tests, placed them in my basket, and headed to the register.

All I wanted to do was cry. Or shake. Or tell myself that this wasn't happening.

I'd had sex once in my life. I couldn't be pregnant.

People didn't get pregnant by doing it just one time.

We had used a condom. And yet, all of that meant nothing because condoms were only marginally good enough. They weren't a hundred percent effective, and I couldn't be on birth control because my family had a propensity to get blood clots. I'd thought we had been safe, but maybe we hadn't been safe enough.

The one time I'd had sex. Now I really was going to throw up again.

The older woman at the register didn't even look

up as she rang up my purchases. I handed over cash, thinking it would be odd if I used a credit card for this. My credit card was my parents', though they didn't have access to the statements. But it still felt like I shouldn't put this on anything that could be read aloud.

Not that they would be able to see the items, but it was all about the what-if.

The clerk gave me my change. I put the leftover dollar in the charity bucket for children and swallowed hard.

I couldn't be a mom.

This wasn't at all what I had planned.

Nothing was.

I wasn't even sure how I made it home. My body was sweat-slick, my hands cold, but nobody else was home. They were all in classes for the day since it was still mid-afternoon. I hadn't even thought about that.

My phone chimed as I walked inside, and I looked down.

Tanner: *On my way.*

Relief spread through me, even as terror hit.

Should I take the test before he arrived? That way, I could make up a situation for why I needed him when it ended up negative. But what if the test was positive? Then I'd have to deal with him.

I wasn't sure what to do, so I sat in my living

room, holding lunch meats, bread, cupcakes, and pregnancy tests, pretending that I knew what I was doing.

Tanner walked in and scowled at me. Why did he look so hot when he scowled? And why was I even thinking about that?

"You didn't lock the door, princess. What the hell is wrong with you?"

I raised my chin, refusing to burst into tears. "Thanks for coming over. We need to talk."

He scowled at the bag in my hand. "So you said. Did you go grocery shopping?"

I clutched the bags tighter to my chest and nodded. "The lunch meat will go bad. I need to put it in the fridge. The cupcakes, too."

"You asked me over to talk about cupcakes?" he said, shaking his head. "You never text me about things like that. But I figured I'd come over since I was home alone. Are you okay?"

I put everything in the fridge, my body covering the rest of the bag so he didn't see the contents.

"I don't know."

"Natalie, I know we didn't talk about what happened, but we can. I know I'm a fucking asshole, but I never wanted to hurt you."

I turned, clutching one of the boxes to my chest. "No, you didn't hurt me. We had rules. One of them was that we weren't going to talk about it again. I get it. Except I think we may *need* to talk about it again."

His eyes got comically big, and he fisted his hands at his sides. "Are you fucking kidding me?"

"I've been sick for a couple of weeks now, and I missed my period. I don't know if I'm supposed to take a test now or call someone. I've never done this before. I had sex *once*, Tanner. This isn't how things are supposed to go. But I didn't want to do this alone. I know we're friends, or at least we pretend to be, so I figured you could stand outside in the hall while I take it. And then it can be negative, and we can never speak about this again."

He moved forward, his hand outstretched, and then he froze. "You're sick?" His voice cracked. This time, a single tear fell down my cheek.

Out of everything he could have said, the first thing was words of worry that I had been sick.

It was so hard not to fall for this man.

"I keep throwing up."

He nodded but moved forward again, brushing the tear away from my cheek. "Okay, we're friends. Always. That's what we said. And I don't go back on what I say. Fuck, Natalie."

I snorted, the curse bringing me out of my funk. "I know."

"This is one of those pee-on-the-stick things? Does

it say pregnant or not? Or am I going to have to look for lines? I kind of want it to be the one that has the words on it."

I reached for the bag and pulled out another pregnancy test. "I got one with lines and one with words. Let's do the words first, just in case."

"Two. We're going to take two." He let out a breath, his chest moving slowly.

"Just in case."

"Sounds like a plan to me. So, I'll stand outside?"

I winced. "You're not going to be inside while I take the test. We're friends, but I don't think we're *that* kind of friends."

"If you're pregnant with my kid, we might become that kind." His eyes widened, his face going pale as soon as he said the words. "Well, shit."

My heart pounded in my ears, and I had a feeling the staccato rhythm matched Tanner's. "Those are good words. Keep those up. But it will be negative. And then we'll never talk about this again. We can go on about our days and be real friends. We're doing great. We haven't even been awkward once."

He raised a brow.

"Okay, maybe a little bit awkward, but this is fine. Now, I'm going to go pee. I'll probably have to drink more water because I keep throwing it up."

"Natalie," he whispered, his voice so caring it made me want to cry.

"I'm fine, really."

"Anyone that says *fine* in that high-pitched voice really isn't," he drawled.

"True. And I'm lying to myself and you. But that *is* fine. And I know I said fine again. Deal with it." I went to the fridge, pulled out a water bottle, and brought the two pregnancy tests with me.

Tanner sighed. "I'm not going to throw this receipt in the trashcan, just in case."

"Yes, evidence."

"Fuck," he muttered again but followed me down the hall.

I turned at the doorway to the bathroom and raised my chin.

"I'll be quick, I hope. And then it's going to be negative, and we can laugh about this."

"Let's think negative thoughts then," he said and grimaced.

I snorted and closed the door to the restroom, grateful that we could find humor in this situation.

Somehow, I did what I needed to do, washed my hands, brushed my teeth, and then opened the door.

He stood there, his arms folded over his chest. His gorgeous arms, ones I was *not* going to notice.

"Well?"

My body shook, and I turned my head towards the test. "Five minutes. Three more to go."

He nodded tightly, and we both stood there as if we hadn't slept together and weren't waiting to find out if our lives were about to be changed. It was awkward.

He cleared his throat, looking as out of sorts as I felt. "Natalie, I don't know what to say."

"Maybe we won't have to say anything. Maybe I just have the flu. Unfortunately, I kept going to school and probably gave it to everybody like the plague."

"We can only hope," he muttered.

My phone chimed, the alarm going off, and we both jumped.

I let out a little squeal, and then Tanner took my hand and squeezed it.

The lifeline he offered brought me back to the here and now. I swallowed hard and looked up at him.

"I don't know what I'm supposed to do."

"We look. You took both tests?"

"I figured it'd be good so we didn't have to wait."

"I've never done this, either, Natalie. I don't know what I'm doing."

"This is good. It's going to be negative, and then we have experience if it ever happens again in the future."

I was rambling at this point, but when I pulled him

into the restroom, squeezing his hand for dear life, I wanted to cry.

I wanted to break down and pretend that this wasn't happening to me. That this was a dream that would one day be over, where I wouldn't have to think about it at all anymore.

Only that wasn't the case.

"You're pregnant," he muttered. I looked up at him and saw that his face was impossibly pale.

"I'm pregnant," I whispered. "How is this happening?"

"I don't fucking know, Natalie. I mean, I *know*, and it was great and everything, but…oh, my God."

"If you're just going to leave me forever and never want to talk about this again and have me do this on my own, can you just go now? Because I'm panicking, and I can't deal with anyone else's emotions. I need to focus on what the hell is going on with me."

He cursed under his breath and then turned me in his arms. My eyes widened, and then he crushed his mouth to mine.

He tasted of sweetness and panic—or maybe that was only me. When he pulled away and rested his forehead against mine, I took a breath. "I don't know what we're going to do. I'm not that guy. I'm going to panic right alongside you, we'll probably fuck this up, and I have no idea what the hell we'll do next, but I'm not going to run."

I looked into his eyes and wanted to believe him. I wanted to believe that he wouldn't leave me alone in this, no matter what happened. Everything was so scary. It was so much. But being overwhelmed helped me believe. I let myself believe in a possible lie. And that was fine.

"Okay," I whispered, then wrapped my arms around his waist as I broke down. Sobs racked my body, and I wondered exactly how this had happened. How was this my life? Tanner crushed me to him, his chin on the top of my head as he rubbed my back with his hand.

We were pregnant. We were having a baby.

Nothing would ever be the same again.

Eight

Tanner

The following week went by in a whirlwind of stress, worry, and secrets. Neither of us had told our roommates what had happened yet. It was too early, at least that's what we had told each other. I still could not believe this was happening.

The girl I had slept with once—using a condom and being as safe as I could possibly be—was pregnant. While I couldn't quite wrap my head around it, and couldn't catch my breath, I knew it had to be a thousand times worse for Natalie.

Her first time had been rough and quick and

spontaneous, and now, we both had to deal with the consequences. Yet, she had to deal with it more than I did. At least, in the sense of it being her body. I wouldn't let her down. Wouldn't run away and hide from my responsibilities. But it was also primarily on her shoulders. I felt like such a fucking dick. The guys would probably beat the shit out of me once they found out, and the girls might end up castrating me. I winced and ran my hand through my hair, looking down at my textbooks. I was supposed to be studying. As if I could actually focus right then—there was no such thing as focus. Not when I was petrified that I had ruined Natalie's life. One moment of need, of want, and she would have to deal with our choices forever.

In the past week, she had gone to her doctor to get another test. We were three for three in officially being pregnant, and we hadn't even discussed what to do. It was hard to do that while keeping secrets from our friends and trying to find time to speak with one another about what had happened.

I had worked three nights this week and the first term paper of the semester was due. Natalie had been just as busy and feeling sick half the time. I knew the girls would likely catch on soon. There was no way they missed how Natalie kept having to run to the restroom.

Only it wasn't my place to tell them. Damn, I was such a fucking idiot.

I was going to be a father. If things progressed as they were, I would be holding a baby that was *ours* in a handful of months. We would be heading into our futures, hopefully with degrees in our hands, but with both of us tied together irrevocably, no matter what became of our so-called relationship. And that was the thing. We didn't *have* a relationship. We were friends, but neither of us had ever said we wanted more than what we already had. Or maybe I just didn't let myself want more. She was Natalie, the rich girl with a future. She could do whatever she wanted, but instead of living on her parents' money, she was going into social work. She would face countless hours at a thankless job and would be excellent at it. Or, at least, she would have been until I ruined her life by getting her pregnant. Now, I didn't know what either of us was going to do. This changed everything. We planned to talk a little bit today; something we hadn't been able to do outside of texts for the past week. We needed to make some plans, make this real rather than some abstract idea of a baby.

I wanted to throw up.

A knock sounded on my bedroom door, and I stiffened, not knowing if I wanted it to be a roommate or Natalie.

"Tanner?" Natalie whispered through the door, and I swallowed hard.

"Door's unlocked. Come in." I got up off the bed and walked towards the door.

She opened it, her bag over her shoulder, and an awkward smile on her face. "Hi. I just realized I don't think I've ever actually been in your bedroom."

And we were having a child together? We definitely weren't doing this in the proper order—not that there *was* an order to changing your life forever.

I stood only a foot in front of her and wanted to reach out and hug her close, tell her everything would be okay even as my heart raced. She had pulled her blond hair over one shoulder, her blue eyes wide as she bit her lip. She wore a sweater that wrapped around her shoulders, and jeans tucked into knee-high boots. She looked classy and sexy. Was I supposed to think a pregnant woman was sexy? I'd never done this before, and I had no idea what I was doing. I would probably mess everything up—something I was getting good at.

"It's my bedroom. Not anything special."

Her lips quirked into a genuine smile, and I cleared my throat. I wasn't sure what to say. I wasn't good at this. I was usually decent while working with people. Despite the fact that I was an asshole a lot of the time, I knew how to talk to other humans. Yet with Natalie, I couldn't. When the guys and I moved into the house, there had been five of us. We had each pulled a Twizzler out of Pacey's hands—a favorite of our British roommate—and the length of the candy rope corresponded to the size of the bedrooms.

When Sanders moved out after being the asshole we discovered he was, we had shifted rooms around a bit so the smallest room was empty for guests. So far, only Miles' little brother had used it, and that was only recently since Miles' parents were finally letting up on the reins a bit when it came to their kids. I hadn't invited my brother out here yet and probably wouldn't, mainly because he was a little too young for that, and it was a bit of a drive. At one point, we had thought we might move Natalie and Nessa into that room, primarily because of Nessa's stalker. But that situation was fixed now, and I hadn't had to sleep under the same roof as Natalie. That was a good thing, especially since I couldn't stop thinking about her.

"I brought my homework, even though I don't think I can actually think about what I need to do with it," she said, pulling me out of my thoughts.

I gestured towards the open books on my desk that I hadn't read a word of today since I couldn't focus, either. "Same here. I finished my part of the group project, and now I wait for everybody not to do theirs."

She cringed. "I have a group paper due soon. *A group paper.* How is that even okay?" she asked as she set her bag down next to my books. "Is it okay if I put these here?" Her voice was so tentative. I let out a curse, and she picked up the bag again.

"It's fine. I can put it in the chair or on the floor, just let me know."

I cursed again, took the bag from her, set it back on the desk, and then cupped her face. Her eyes widened for a moment, and I placed my mouth on hers, needing her taste, wanting to soothe myself.

She sank into me, her hands going to my chest, digging in, not pushing me away.

"Oh," she whispered.

"Oh, is a good word." I sighed. "You're welcome to put your shit anywhere you want." I cringed. "I don't mean that in an asshole way. I promise."

"I believe you." She blinked up at me. "So, we're going to keep kissing then?"

"We can. But we should probably talk."

"You're right. Talking first. I just keep wondering why you keep kissing me."

"Because I want to?" I asked, and she rolled her eyes as she stepped away.

"That might be a good enough reason if we weren't having a baby." Her eyes widened as she said it, as if she couldn't believe the words had come out of her mouth. And, honestly, I was right there with her.

She put her hand over her still-flat stomach, and my mouth went dry.

"Jesus," I whispered.

"That sounds about right. What are we going to do, Tanner?" she asked softly.

"Let's take a seat."

"Is it okay if we don't sit on the bed?" she asked as she looked at the small loveseat I had in the corner.

"Yeah. Sitting on the bed with you will be a little difficult."

"Really?" she asked, surprise in her voice.

I ran my hand through my hair and couldn't help but watch the way her gaze went to the muscles on my arms.

Well, then.

"Natalie, let's just get this out of the way."

She swallowed hard. "Okay."

"I want you. I've wanted you from the first time I saw you. You're beautiful, intelligent, and funny—or whatever order you need that to be in. I like you as a person, and I don't regret the fact that we slept together. I can't because it was fucking amazing, although the circumstances of everything is twisting me up inside. I liked having sex with you. And if we weren't in the middle of whatever the fuck we're doing now with you being pregnant, I may want to have sex with you again."

"So, we're just going to be blunt then?"

"Being secretive and sneaky isn't my thing."

She snorted.

"What?"

"Being secretive and sneaky is totally your thing. You don't tell anybody what you do for a living. You act growly around anybody who gets too close. We know nothing about you other than the fact that you lived in a small town over an hour away from here. You say that you're the bad boy from the wrong side of the tracks or whatever the hell you said that one time you were drunk with Miles, but we know nothing about you, Tanner. You're good at pushing people away. So, yes, you are the secretive guy. And that's fine. You don't need to tell us everything about yourself, but don't pretend you're an open book. People who say they are, are the most closed-off."

I scowled and shook my head. "That's not true."

"It is. And I'm not saying you should tell me everything. Okay, maybe you should tell me some things because I would love to know more about you, considering we are having a child together, but you don't need to bare your soul to every single human you meet. You also don't need to hide in the corner and pretend the world is against you."

"I don't understand you," I whispered.

"I don't understand me, either; it's sort of why we're at school. To figure out who we are."

"I thought we were at school to get degrees so we could get fucking jobs."

"That's also true. But there's this whole time in your twenties when you're supposed to find the path you want to take and change your mind. Some of us may have the privilege of changing our minds more than once, but look at us. We're pregnant. There's a baby growing inside me. That completely changes any path I thought I would be on."

Guilt swamped me. "You're not going to do this alone. I mean, I know we're not together or anything, and I don't know what I have to offer, but I won't just leave you."

Tears filled her eyes, and I felt like an asshole all over again. "Natalie," I began, and she shook her head.

"No, every time you say something like that, it only makes me weepy. But in a good way."

"Weepy's good?"

"I know you're close with your mother. You have to understand that."

I cringed. "I used to be close with my mother. Not these days."

She opened her mouth to say something but then

stopped. Maybe she was right. Maybe I wasn't that open book I pretended to be.

Shit.

"I'm keeping it, by the way," she whispered, and I blinked.

"You mean…?" I whispered, pointing to her stomach.

"Yes. That. I thought about my choices. This will change everything, and I have no idea what I'm doing. My family will likely hate me and try to punish me for it, but I'm not going to put this baby up for adoption or anything like that."

I nodded before reaching out to tuck her hair behind her ear. "I'm here. I guess I need to make plans."

"My parents are judgmental. They're going to want me to get married and come home and raise the baby with them. And go with every plan they make for me."

I winced. "They can't make you do anything."

"I know that, Tanner. But they're very forceful. And I love them. I know it sounds like I don't sometimes, but I do. They love me, too, and only want what's best for me, even if they keep trying to set me up on dates with near-forty-year-old men."

I narrowed my eyes. "Excuse me?" I growled.

"It's nothing. Seriously. I'm not dating any of them.

And no one's going to want to date me out of that subset once they find out I'm pregnant."

"With my kid," I snarled.

"Yes. Something we did together. That we're going to have to deal with."

"My mom will probably be ecstatic, mostly because she loves babies. She wanted more after my brother and me, but then Dad died, and she pulled away from everything." I swallowed hard, and Natalie reached out and brushed her fingers along my jaw—just a sweet caress from someone who cared. I had to wonder why we just clicked.

"I'm sorry."

"He got hit in an IED blast in Afghanistan. Times were tough for a while, but the scholarship for school really helped. And then, well, you know what job I do now to send money back home. Mom needs help, so I'm doing what I can."

"You're a good son."

"I don't think she'd feel that way if she found out I'm a stripper who got the girl who isn't my girlfriend pregnant."

She flinched. "That's going to put a bit of a damper on everything."

"She'll get over it quick, though—mostly because she does like babies. But the guy she's currently dating? He's going to be a real asshole about it."

"What do you mean?"

I hadn't wanted to bring this up. I didn't know why I did. There was no going back now, though. "My dad's friend practically moved in on my mom right after the funeral. He's an asshole and is the reason I moved out as quickly as I did. They're not married yet, but I know it's only a matter of time. You just can tell with those things, you know? He's a fucking loser, and while I don't think he's violent, he probably could be. You know when you can just feel that?"

She bit her lip and nodded. "I do. I'm sorry."

"Me, too. So, that's who I am. The kid who grew up on food stamps for most of his life and strips for money so my mom doesn't have to remain on them. It sucks, but I plan on getting a good job to make up for all of that. I have a line on a company—through Dillon's connections, actually. They are going to hire me right out of college as long as I keep my grades up. I can use them as my internship."

"The Montgomerys?" she asked, grinning.

I rolled my eyes. "It seems like everybody knows the Montgomerys."

"It's true. And that's great. See, there're plans. And this doesn't have to change that." She pointed to her stomach, and I scowled.

"This changes everything."

"It changes most things, but you getting a job after

school won't change." She let out a breath. "And I'm going to finish school, as well. I might need to take some time off afterwards to get through the first couple of years of this baby's life since my plan to go directly into social work the way I wanted might not work with a crying infant at home."

"Natalie," I whispered.

"No, it's fine. And I know you're going to hate this idea, but I do have a trust fund. I have several, actually."

I frowned, not liking the sharp tug of annoyance I felt at that. It wasn't Natalie's fault that she came from money, but I hated that she would be able to provide for herself and our child without any help from me.

"Don't get that look on your face. You said you wanted to be here, so be here. I'm going to work. I'll finish school and find my path. I don't know how it'll all settle. And I don't know what my family will say—or even yours. I don't know how our friends will react, and I don't know what you and I will be to each other while we're doing this, but I know I'm privileged. I know that I have more avenues for this pregnancy than many others would. I don't want to think about all of that right now. I don't want to deal with every single detail. All I've been doing this past week is dealing with every minute issue in my life. Can't I just have like a moment to breathe?"

I pushed away all thoughts of money and futures and nodded before leaning down to kiss her. She froze for an instant, and I was suddenly afraid I had done the wrong thing.

"Is this smart?" she whispered against my lips, and I shook my head.

"Not really. But why the hell shouldn't we complicate things further?" I growled.

She nodded against my lips before kissing me back, and I wrapped my arms around her.

I had no idea what the hell we were going to do, or what might happen to us in the next moment, but if we could pretend for just these few seconds, then…why not? The part of me that had always wanted her wasn't going away anytime soon.

And now, we would be forever connected in a way that neither of us had planned.

So, maybe I could pretend for just this instant, and later we could deal with the consequences. Something that we had to face with every turn.

Nine

Natalie

I sat in the large living room and did my best to act as if I weren't panicking. And yet, panic was pretty much the only emotion I could focus on. There was fear, anxiety, and a dash of excitement, but mostly panic.

Tanner stood on the other side of the room, talking with Pacey, but I could tell his head wasn't in the game. Instead, he seemed to only nod along as if he were stressed out like I was. I didn't blame him since I was right there with him. I couldn't understand how this was happening. Only, of course, I did. We were here to tell the roommates what had happened. It had been three weeks since we found out. Three weeks of hiding and making plans that weren't really plans. How could you make plans when everything was so up in the air? Grad schools and jobs after this final semester were necessary, yet I couldn't focus on any of it when I knew that things could change on a dime.

We needed to tell my family. We needed to tell *his* family, but it wasn't happening yet. We wanted to make the three-month mark before we told our parents and altered everything. But we also knew that we couldn't hide things from the roommates. I didn't know what it said about the connections we had made that we could so easily tell our friends and not our families, but perhaps it made sense because we had chosen that family.

"Do you want to tell us why you asked us here?" Nessa said after a few more minutes, and I swallowed hard. Pacey gave me a look, and everybody began looking between Tanner and me, their brows raised.

"You owe me five dollars," Nessa said, and Miles shook his head. He pushed his glasses up his nose, a small smile crinkling his face.

"You can't let them know we were betting on whether they were doing it or not."

I knew my face drained of color, and I looked across the room at Tanner. He cleared his throat as he made his way to my side. I sat in a wingback chair, slightly apart from the others, and hoped they hadn't noticed.

I needed to be able to think, though. And I couldn't do that if I was sitting next to everyone, trying to have a normal conversation that was anything but normal.

Pacey leaned forward and put his hand on my shoulder, squeezing, and Elise smiled. "I guess that's four for four. That is why you asked us here, right? To tell us you guys are dating?"

"It does make it kind of neat," Dillon added as he ran his hands down Elise's arm.

Pacey cleared his throat. "Should I be the one who asks when this happened and how serious it is?"

Mackenzie looked up at Pacey and snorted. "You know that's my line."

"I'm just saving you the trouble, darling." He leaned down and kissed her softly, and I gritted my teeth, doing my best to catch my breath.

"It's relatively new," Tanner said, and I looked up at him, my eyes wide.

He sighed and leaned down, brushing his lips against mine. "Well? It is."

"Yes, it is."

"What's going on?" Elise asked, her voice suddenly somber. "This seems a little more serious than you just telling us you're dating. Not that dating isn't serious. But…I don't know, talk to us."

My mouth went dry, and Tanner leaned forward and then handed me my water. I hadn't even asked him to do it, yet he seemed to know what I needed.

Why was he so great? We spent as much time together as possible, the two of us the only ones in on our secret. I had a doctor's appointment coming up, and we needed to figure out how to become parents. But we also did our best to pretend that it wasn't happening. We made pretend plans and went back to work. Tanner was still stripping, and I was still doing charity work.

And, all the while, we had been lying to everyone and acting as if our lives hadn't been irrevocably altered.

"I'm pregnant," I blurted, and Tanner's hand squeezed my shoulder so tightly, I was afraid it might leave bruises. He let me go quickly as if he realized what he had done, and I swallowed hard.

Everyone was silent for so long, I was afraid I hadn't actually said anything.

Perhaps I only imagined saying the words. The silence was deafening. And yet, Tanner had reacted, so I must have said the words aloud.

I was pregnant.

This wasn't how I'd expected my life to go. I had

thought that I would have children someday—much later in life. Perhaps even nearing my thirties, once I was truly settled into my career and found the perfect husband, and we were settled for just a bit longer. I wanted to be secure in who I was and the dreams I had before bringing a child into the world. I wanted to help other children who didn't have the footing they needed to thrive.

"It's not April yet, is it?" Nessa asked before letting out a hollow laugh that didn't ring true to my ears. "You can't be serious. We didn't even know if you were genuinely dating. When did this happen? *How* did this happen? And why is my voice getting so high?"

"Pregnant? How did that happen so quickly?" Elise sputtered before looking at Mackenzie.

Mackenzie just shook her head. "Are you okay?"

I didn't know if they were saying all the right things, but they were saying everything that had gone through my mind already.

"What the fuck, man?" Dillon growled, looking over my shoulder at Tanner.

"It happened. We're dealing with it. We haven't told our families yet, but we thought it would be good to tell you since Natalie has morning sickness, and we don't want to keep secrets anymore."

I looked up at him and then tugged him down so he sat on the edge of the chair. I tangled my fingers with his and squeezed. He looked down at our hands, and the tension in his shoulders eased ever so slightly.

Then Miles spoke, the tension rising once again. "You're having a baby. Okay, then. I didn't expect this. I mean…*Natalie*?"

I looked at all of them then and knew I likely wasn't explaining this correctly. If I had, they would be confused right along with me, but the complete and real confusion it almost hurt to hear wouldn't be there.

"I don't want to say it was an accident because bringing life into the world can't be that, but it definitely wasn't planned." They all looked at me as if I might be going insane. And maybe I was. "Tanner and I aren't handling this well, but we're trying to. We're not together—or maybe we are. That is probably an essential aspect that we'll need to deal with before this baby is born or before we tell our parents what's going on. But we're doing this. We had sex. We used a condom. And, apparently, condoms don't work all the time."

Tanner cursed under his breath. "We were safe. These things happen. We're pregnant."

"You keep saying 'we,' and yet she's the one having the baby," Nessa exclaimed and put her hand over her mouth. "I'm sorry. I like you, Tanner, I'm just really confused and alarmed right now."

"It's fine," he muttered, but it wasn't fine.

They were all acting as if he had done something nefarious. But then again, maybe they thought he had.

"We all know I was a virgin. And now I'm not. Things happen."

Tanner put his hand over his face and groaned. "Natalie."

I looked up at him. "What? Why aren't you saying anything? I'm terrified, and I want my friends to be by my side. I know they want to be. They're just sitting there in shock like I am. I need to be happy about this because…yay, we're having a baby. But, oh my God. I'm twenty-two years old. I'm not ready to be a mom. Still, we're going to be parents. And I need my friends. Okay?"

They all moved in then and hugged me hard. I didn't even realize I was crying until Tanner pulled my back to his chest, and the others were wiping my tears. "Congratulations," Elise said, wiping her tears from her face. "You're going to be a mom."

"Out of all of us, you'll probably be the best mom," Mackenzie said. "Which is good since you're doing it first."

"First?" Pacey said, practically squeaking out the word.

That made me snort. "Look at me, trying to lead the charge. We don't know what we're doing, but I would love for you guys to be at our sides while we figure it out, because we're still in college. I'm going to finish my degree since my due date is after graduation. I don't know what'll happen after that. Neither of us does. If you guys could just not judge us and help us instead, that would be wonderful."

"We're not judging you," Dillon said, and I froze, noticing Tanner doing the same.

"I see. That's me, the asshole. It's fine. I'm good at being the asshole."

"Tanner," I whispered.

"That's not what I meant..." Dillon began before Tanner cut him off.

"No, it's okay. I get it. I knew what I was doing, you didn't. And even though we used a condom, it didn't work. That's on me. So, blame me, hit me, call me fuckface, I don't care. Natalie is not doing this alone. I'm going to be here. But for now, I think I know when I'm not wanted." He walked out, leaving me standing there surrounded by my friends. I couldn't help but wonder what had just happened.

"What the hell was that?" Pacey asked, blinking. "We didn't blame him. We're not blaming anyone. We're just three steps behind whatever the fuck is happening."

"Really? You guys were glaring at him. You did that. You treated him like a jerk or like he took advantage of me. He didn't. I wanted him just as much as he wanted me—probably more if I'm honest."

"Natalie, darling, you were a virgin," Mackenzie whispered.

My eyes narrowed to slits. "You're right. But so was Corinne. And she died. Remember that? She died without ever having sex. I did not want to die a virgin. I did not want to graduate college without having sex. I wasn't waiting till marriage. I was waiting for the right time. And that was the perfect time."

"Natalie," Elise whispered, and I shook my head.

"I love you all. We told you because we thought it would be great if you were by our sides as we made the important decisions. I've always been there for you when you guys needed to talk things out. When you started with your relationships and wanted to share about classes or your families, I was there to do my best to be your shoulder. Now, I need you to be mine. And Tanner's."

"We didn't mean to blame him," Dillon said. "I know it looked like that, and maybe it sounded that way, but he's our friend. He's a good guy. We know he would never take advantage of you."

"Then make sure he knows that. Tell him you're sorry and deal with it. Now, I need to find him because I'm scared. And he's never once treated me as less than."

"We're not doing that, are we?" Nessa asked, her eyes brimming with tears.

"You're not. I promise. You made Tanner feel like that, though. Even if it wasn't your intention, you did. All six of you are in healthy and strong relationships. Tanner and I aren't. I don't know what we are exactly, and that's scary. I have no idea what I'm doing. And I'm going to need my friends. So, take a breath, talk amongst yourselves, get out any random whatever the fuck you need to about the fact that we are having a baby, and then come to us when you're ready. I need to find Tanner. The father of my child." And with that, I grabbed my bag and turned to follow Tanner.

My friends hadn't meant to say anything wrong or to act the way they did. After all, we *had* surprised them. Only it didn't matter just then. I needed to find Tanner. I needed everything to be okay. Because if he wasn't there to be my rock, then I would have to be the strong one, and I wasn't ready for that.

I was afraid if I didn't grow a spine or find my footing soon, I would never be the rock I needed to be.

And we were running out of time.

Ten

Tanner

I paced around Natalie's driveway, annoyed at myself for coming here. I could have gone anywhere. I could have gone to the club, to school, to a fucking coffee shop. But, no, I had run away from my problems like I did every single fucking time and came right to Natalie's place.

As if I were waiting for her. But I shouldn't be. Just because it was within walking distance didn't mean this was the place for me.

I hated myself just a little bit then, and I knew that I only had myself to blame for it. Of course, the others *would* blame me for what had happened with Natalie. I blamed myself. I'd given in to temptation, and now Natalie would have to deal with the consequences. Yes, I would be there. I would do what I could. But she and I were barely figuring out if we wanted to be in a relationship. And I didn't have to go through the pregnancy, birth, hormonal issues, or anything else that had to do with having a baby. That was all her. I could merely stand by and tell her I'd be there for her—even if that wasn't enough.

That was all on her. And I hated myself a little bit.

I looked up at the small, two-story house the girls lived in and scowled. I didn't like the place. It was rundown and not as big as the last home they'd lived in. When we helped move the girls in after they had left their last house, I had told the guys that I wasn't fond of the place. While they had all agreed that it wasn't as good as the last one, real estate was in high demand here. It wasn't like they could do anything about it.

I sighed and figured maybe I should go to the library or something. I had work to do, and if I was going to skip out on my responsibilities, I might as well do *something*. I had to work later, but I was on the late shift, so it wasn't as if I needed to be there right now. The boss didn't like it if we hung out at the club when we weren't on duty. It took away from the people on stage, according to him. While I sometimes agreed with it, I kind of wished I could go and talk to JC. The other man would be able to help me through this new hell going on in my brain.

Footsteps sounded behind me, and I turned and scowled.

"I can't believe you just left like that."

I blinked at Natalie. "Of course, I did. I wasn't wanted. What are you doing here?"

"Are you serious? I live here."

"Fine," I grumbled, knowing I didn't have a leg to stand on here.

This was her place. I was the intruder.

"Come inside. The others are going to stay away for a bit and give me some space."

"Natalie."

"No. I'm angry."

"You have every right to be angry. I left. I was an asshole."

She turned on me as she stood on the doorstep, her eyes wide. "You were an asshole, but you don't need to apologize to me for it."

I blinked, confused. "What?"

"You don't need to apologize to me. They treated you like crap just now. Of course, you're going to be angry about it. You didn't need to stand there and have them act like it was all your fault."

"It *was* my fault," I grumbled.

She scowled at me, huffed out a breath, and turned to unlock the door. I had installed the lock a few months ago, and it was holding for now, but they needed a new door. However, I knew the landlord wouldn't do anything about it. The whole place was decrepit, and the power went out more often than it should. The electricians they had gotten out here to take a look swore the place was up to code, but I didn't know if I quite believed that. I was truly afraid that something bad would happen one day, and I wouldn't be here to help.

Not that the girls should call me. After all, I was the guy who took advantage of sweet, innocent virgins and got them pregnant.

"Stop," she growled.

"I kind of like it when you growl," I teased, not even aware that I was going to say the words until they were already out of my mouth.

She narrowed her eyes at me. "Yes, you're adorable. Seriously, though, Tanner. Stop acting like it's your fault. We both decided to have sex. We were careful. However, we were not careful enough. It is not your fault that I'm pregnant. It's *our* fault. And we both decided to deal with the consequences."

"And yet, I was the one with the experience. You weren't."

"You don't have experience in being a father or

dealing with pregnancy. Yet you're the one giving me crackers and holding my hair back. And all while I couldn't tell anyone else that I'm having a baby. You're the one gaining experience in dealing with a pregnant friend or girlfriend or whatever the fuck we are to each other while going to college."

I blinked. "You curse often. When you do, it always surprises me."

"Shit, fuck, damn, every other curse word you want to think of." She smirked. "I'm allowed to say them. I'm having a baby."

"So, you're going to curse in front of the kid?" I asked, knowing that I was losing my damn mind.

She huffed out a breath. "You exhaust me, Tanner."

I sighed and tugged her through the house. She had said that the roommates would give us some time, but I didn't know if I believed that. I figured either they would come here and force her away from me so they could ensure that she was truly safe from my nefarious purposes, or they would come and want to apologize. That wouldn't give us enough time to talk things out and figure out what the hell we were going to do. We needed privacy. She let me pull her down the hall and up the stairs to her room. I could have propped her over my shoulder and carried her, but I wasn't sure what that might do to the baby. I was only partially through the baby book that Natalie had given me, and I was a little afraid to finish it. It was a lot more detailed than expected.

"Okay, you've locked me in my room with you. The last time we locked ourselves away like this, *this* happened." She pointed to her still-flat stomach, and I shook my head.

"We didn't lock the door last time. Hell, we didn't even close it."

She blushed. "That's true."

Anybody could have walked in.

"I know that's supposed to be bad, but it's kind of hot."

I groaned, my dick standing at attention. "Are you serious right now?"

"I don't know if I'm serious right now. I don't know anything."

"Neither do I, but the roommates are pissed off. What the hell are your parents going to think?"

"My parents have nothing to do with this," she said, raising her chin. I laughed outright.

"You're serious? That's what you're going with?"

"They don't have anything to do with this baby."

"They're going to have everything to do with it. They're going to blame me for daring to touch their pretty little princess."

"Fuck you, Tanner. I'm not some spoiled little rich girl. Get over yourself."

"And I'm not the poor boy from the wrong side of the tracks. Although, sometimes, it sure does feel like it, doesn't it?"

We stared at each other, and then she leaned forward and put her finger against my chest. She pushed slightly. I could barely feel it. "Cute."

"Screw you."

"We already did that. And look what happened."

"Tanner. Seriously. We're going to be co-parents. And yet you keep kissing me. I don't know where we are in our relationship or what's going on, and I'm scared. I need you to be on my side here. To be the sane one."

I blinked. "You want me to be the sane one?"

"Yes. You are brilliant and caring and can usually help anybody in your circle without them even asking. So, help yourself. Help me. I'm freaking out, and I need you."

"What do you need me for?"

"To be here. To help me. You're right. My parents will probably disown me or do whatever the hell they want when they realize that I'm pregnant at my age. We're not married. I need you to protect me if your mother calls me a whore and throws things at me."

I snorted. "My mother would never do that."

"I don't know that, do I? You never speak about her."

"I don't know what to say. We weren't dating before, Natalie. And I don't talk about my family. We're doing this ass-backwards."

"We are. So, let's try to make it frontwards."

"That makes no sense."

"I know that. Which is why you need to deal with my crazy hormones."

"Do women get crazy hormones this early in a pregnancy?" I asked, blinking.

"I don't know. But we need to stop fighting. We can't fight and be parents."

Parents. Jesus. We were going to be parents. I wasn't even sure how to take care of myself. How were we supposed to take care of a baby?

"Maybe I shouldn't be a dad," I mumbled.

"Maybe you shouldn't have fucked me." She raised her chin, pressing those pouty little lips together, and I held back a groan.

"You know, I kind of like that word coming out of your mouth." If I could distract her, maybe we wouldn't have to deal with the seriousness. That seemed to be all we had been doing since we found out. We were trying to make plans for a future that was already more than uneasy.

"You like that word coming out of my mouth, yet

you're not going to do anything about it?" she asked, surprising me.

I threw back my head and laughed. "I think I can. But didn't we both say it would complicate things?"

"You claimed me in front of your friends. You're not going to claim me here?"

"When the hell did you get so brazen?"

"I always have been. Just because I was a virgin doesn't mean I hid behind that status. I'm no longer a virgin. Clearly."

"I don't want to take advantage of you."

She pushed at my chest again with that cute little finger.

"You're not taking advantage if I'm willing to give."

"So, what does this mean?"

"It means I want you to kiss me. I want you to let me forget about everything for just an instant, and then we'll continue our plans for our careers, lives, and figure out what we're going to do when we can't hide this pregnancy anymore."

"So, you're going to panic with me?"

"If panicking means you're going to kiss me? Yes."

Knowing it was a bad idea, I stood still for just an instant. But then I couldn't wait any longer. I liked her. I had for a very long time. And that was the problem. I liked her enough that I wouldn't be able to hold back if she asked me to kiss her. Like now. I would do anything for her. I was just now realizing that was true and had been the case since I first met her.

And that was a problem.

For later.

For now, I leaned down and brushed my lips against hers.

She moaned, and I wrapped my arms around her body.

"Is sex still okay this early in the pregnancy?"

She sighed against my lips and raked her nails down my chest. My cock hardened at the touch. "Did you not read that book?"

"It was a little too graphic for me."

"Poor Tanner. Afraid of seeing a vagina?"

"Please, don't ever say that again. Those images were not something I was used to."

"Same here. And I'm scared. But I don't want to think about it right now. We'll talk about where we'll live and how we're going to support ourselves later. For now, let's just pretend."

"I can do that," I whispered and kissed her harder. Her hands moved down my chest and then up under my shirt to touch skin. I moaned and deepened the kiss before backing her to the bed.

She was wearing another dress today, and I couldn't help but groan at the sight.

"I swear you wear these just to tease me."

"Maybe I do."

My gaze shot to hers. "Are you serious?"

"I've wanted you for a long time, Tanner. That's not going to change."

"Okay, then."

I knew it might change. Once she figured out exactly who I was and where I came from, she'd probably walk away. She'd say that we would do this together, but that wouldn't be the case. She had so many more resources than I did. She didn't need me.

For right now, she said that she did. So, maybe I'd be the asshole and give in. Take advantage of the moment.

I slowly lifted her dress over her hips and looked up at her from the edge of the bed. "Pull your straps down and cup your breasts. I want to see you play with your nipples."

Her mouth parted, and she nodded, doing as I instructed. She looked so fucking sexy. Her breasts were far too big for her tiny hands, and it made me moan, my dick pressing hard into my zipper.

She slid her hands over her breasts and arched her back.

"You're so fucking beautiful."

She didn't say anything, just moaned, and I

grinned before leaning forward to slowly slide her panties to the side, exposing her.

"Already so wet for me, baby."

"I feel like I'm always wet around you."

"Good, because I'm always hard around you."

She looked up, pausing in her attention on her breasts. "Really?"

"Yes, really. I always have a fucking hard-on when you're around. That's part of the problem."

"So, why didn't you kiss me before?"

I sighed and kissed the inside of her thigh. "Before, you were off-limits. And I was dating people, remember?"

She nodded. "I remember."

"Plus, I don't share unless it's willingly and part of the relationship. I'm not sharing you, Natalie. Whatever happens with us, I don't share."

I met her gaze, willing her to understand. She nodded and parted her lips again. I leaned forward and licked her. She groaned, her head falling back. I spread her, licking her clit, flicking my tongue against the nub. Her whole body shuddered, and I pressed my hands against her thighs, spreading her wide.

I continued to lick and suck, to tease, and when I slowly probed her entrance with a finger, she shook, her pussy clamping around me.

I pressed my thumb against her clit, spearing her with another finger, and she came, her pussy gripping me like a vise. I grinned, lapping at her, and then I stood as she slowly lay back, her dress around her waist, her panties still pushed to the side, and her eyes wide.

"Whoa."

"I like that."

"But you're still clothed."

"I can fix that."

I toed off my shoes and stripped off my shirt before shucking my pants.

"I still can't believe that fit inside me," she commented, and I froze.

I looked down at my cock, squeezed the base, and held back a laugh. "Okay, then. You do say the best things."

"I say the most awkward things. But thank you for thinking so."

I shook my head before leaning down and stripping off the rest of her clothes. She was naked on the bed, all sweet curves and sin, and I was going to hell. I would have one hell of a good time on the way down, though.

I hovered over her, kissing her, and then frowned. "We both took tests. We're clean."

"And you can't get me pregnant again."

The thought of being bare inside her nearly made

me come, and I slid my cock between her folds. She moaned, widening her legs more. "So, no condom?"

"No condom," I whispered and then kissed her.

She wrapped her arms around me, her fingers scraping down my back, and I smiled. She loved claiming me like that, just a slight mark that would go away, but it was a claim, nonetheless.

And it was a damn good thing because I wanted to claim her. I spread her thighs and then slid inside, her wet heat enveloping me. We both let out a moan before I captured her lips and began to move. She arched into me, meeting me thrust for thrust as I sucked on her neck, her breasts, leaving little marks just like she was doing to me. I turned over onto my back, and she positioned herself over me, riding me. She looked at me for a second as if unsure, and I remembered that she had never done this before. I would have to teach her.

That thought nearly sent me over the edge. I slid my hands over Natalie's hips and arched into her, thrusting from below as she rolled her hips. The sensation robbed me of breath, and I groaned, shaking. When she arched her back, rolling her hips as if lost in ecstasy, I pounded into her harder, needing more. Her whole body pinkened, her nipples hardening as she came, her pussy clamping around my dick. I followed her over, filling her. She fell on top of me, whispering my name, and I held back doing the same.

I couldn't say her name. I couldn't do anything to bring her closer. I was already afraid that I had fallen in love with Natalie the first time I met her. Being with her wasn't good for either of us. She would eventually see the true me, and when that happened, she would leave.

So, I couldn't let myself think I had fallen. I couldn't let her know I had fallen. Because if I did, she'd break me.

What was worse, I was afraid I might break her.

No matter the connection we shared.

Eleven

Natalie

I slid down Tanner's body and smiled up at him, the lazy half-asleep grin he gave me making my heart hurt. It had been over two months of us pretending that we were doing this with clear eyes and unbroken hearts, and I did my best to remember our promise to each other.

We'd walk away if it became too much, but we'd never leave the child we'd created.

It had been four months since Tanner had first taken me and changed our lives, and now here I was, doing my best to pretend I wasn't falling in love with the kind man with me. He might call himself broken, the bad boy, or any other derogatory term he could come up with, but that wasn't who I saw.

Only I couldn't let him know that I could see beneath the surface.

If I did, he'd likely walk away from me, yet stay in my life because he was that good of a man.

It would hurt to be near him and not be *with* him, so I didn't let him see my feelings. I didn't let him see how I fell harder for him with each passing doctor's appointment. Or when he held me close as I cried happy tears about getting the paid internship for the summer. They'd even understood that I was having a baby and wouldn't be able to start until later. It was the perfect job and a promise of something more.

I didn't let Tanner know that my heart nearly burst every time he put his hands on my stomach while reading the baby books. He put his whole soul into becoming the man he thought he needed to be for our child's future. He worked long hours, passed all his exams with flying colors, and was nearly a four-point-oh for his entire college career. He had a job lined up with Montgomery Inc. when he finished school and made things work. We wouldn't have to leave the state or figure out who would follow their dream. Things were falling into place. At least, when it came to our respective futures and ensuring that our child had a support system.

And I was so afraid if something changed between us, I'd end up broken in the end. He'd leave because he hadn't meant to stay. We might be sleeping together, but we hadn't talked about who we were to one another. We'd both done our best not to speak of it. He'd said that he wouldn't let me raise our child alone, which was as much of a commitment as we allowed ourselves.

The fact that we continued sleeping together was almost an afterthought. Something we were good at, that distracted us so we didn't have to discuss anything further. We were having a baby yet doing everything we could to ignore the reality of our situation by pretending that going through checklists of what to do when becoming a parent would help. We'd fallen into a relationship but hadn't set boundaries. Nothing felt real, even though I *wanted* it to be real.

Somehow, I'd allowed myself to believe that this *could* be real.

Only, he would move on.

He had to.

We'd only meant for it to be one night. As a distraction. I wasn't meant to be his forever.

"Why are you frowning at my dick? Is something

wrong?" Tanner tugged gently on my ponytail as he spoke, worry in his tone.

I looked up at him, my hand still around the base of his cock, the tip near my mouth. I smiled, doing my best to push all thoughts of what could be out of my mind. "Just wondering if I should go hard and fast or tease slightly before I ride you for our morning fun," I lied.

Tanner met my gaze, and I knew he saw something I didn't want him to see. So, I did my best to do what I'd done the past two years I'd known him. I lied. I hid all feelings for the man I was falling for and pretended that we weren't making a mistake by continuing this farce while the seriousness of our situation lay in shattered remains around us.

Instead of letting him speak again, I swallowed the tip of his cock, hollowing my cheeks as I took more of him into my mouth. Tanner groaned before moving my head where he wanted me. I sucked him, playing gently with his balls with my free hand.

In the past two months since we'd started this, he'd taught me how to please him, and I'd learned how he *loved* to pleasure me. We might not know what would happen in the next few months, but we'd learned that, at least in bed—or on the couch, in the shower, or the car—we were combustible and compatible.

Tanner shifted his hips, and I took him deeper, humming along his length. Before I could blink, he lifted me and spun me around. I let out a groan as he put me on all fours, my knees on the edge of the bed as he stood behind me.

"I can't wait," he growled, and then he was inside me. I came suddenly, the bliss stealing all thought.

It felt as if he were all around me, touching me, making me feel and breathe and gasp. I couldn't focus on anything but him, and I knew if I weren't careful, the frayed tether between us would snap, and I would lose part of myself along the way. But I didn't care.

I was falling for Tanner Hagen, my friend, the father of my child, and the man I shouldn't love. But I didn't care. Not when he made me feel like this. Like I was the center of his world. So many people relied on him, even if he didn't think so. And that meant that, no matter what, he would always break pieces of himself for others, never leaving anything behind.

I promised myself I'd pull those pieces together to protect him if he let me. Only I wasn't sure he would ever let me in enough to make that happen.

It didn't matter, not in that instant. In that moment, we were in our personal reality, and it was everything.

He pounded into me, both of us shaking, and when he came, filling me to the point I knew we'd likely both burst from sensation, I cried his name. Suddenly, I was on my back again as he slid home once more, clearly needing to be inside me even after his orgasm just because he wanted to kiss and hold me.

Yes, I was falling in love with Tanner Hagen.

And it was the only mistake I knew I'd never regret.

At four months along, I couldn't hide my pregnancy any longer. I'd ballooned seemingly overnight, and now I had a slight baby bump that shouted to the world that I was pregnant. I'd stood in the mirror that morning after my shower with Tanner, the two of us staring at our reflections. We were both naked, and only the fact that my body had changed and altered the fake reality we'd made had torn my gaze from the glory that was Tanner without clothes.

Now, I stood in a wrap dress, my small baby bump barely showing. The shape of the dress hid it at most angles, though I knew that as the weeks passed, I wouldn't be able to hide it anymore. But my professors knew, my future employer knew, and my friends knew —at least, the roommates from both homes. I hadn't told my other friends from high school, nor had I told my parents. I hated the idea that I was hiding things from them, but I still wasn't sure how they would react.

I wanted a concrete plan and maybe something

more than a simple we're-working-it-out code to my relationship with Tanner before I told my parents they would be grandparents far before they were ready. I had gone to a few dinners at my parents' house and dealt with more setups that hadn't gone anywhere. Tanner had grumbled about those, but he understood because, while we hadn't officially committed to one another because that would require talking to each other, we also both knew that my mother wouldn't stop trying to set me up on dates until I was married and pregnant.

Just not pregnant and semi-alone.

I would have to tell them soon, though. My body had changed enough that they would be able to tell the next time they saw me. Telling them that I didn't want a glass of wine with dinner because I had to drive and had coursework to deal with would only go so far for so long. While none of it was a lie, it neared the edges of one, and that was enough for me.

Today, however, the girls I had grown up with were about to find out. They were observant. They would know. When I was at the wedding a few weeks prior, I hadn't been showing at all yet, and no one noticed I hadn't been drinking because everybody was doing so many other things.

Now, though, it would be different. We were all going out to brunch, and that meant mimosas.

Mimosas I wouldn't be able to drink. And I didn't think the whole schoolwork and driving excuse would work this time.

My parents weren't going to find out from them, though. Because no matter what happened between us, the girls and I had a code. We did not tell our overbearing parents anything, not even through the grapevine. That included arrests, pregnancy scares, the first time one of our friends had gotten engaged, and even a truancy violation.

We kept our secrets, or at least we had. Though these women weren't my best friends anymore. So, I just had to hope that they wouldn't send my parents into a fit because they found out through rumor and hearsay rather than hearing it from me.

I walked into the upscale café and smiled at the maître d', who recognized me and gestured to my table. We used to come here every Sunday as a group, but since we weren't roommates anymore and people were getting married and moving on in their lives, these get-togethers were rare.

Janice was the first one to notice me. She gave me a little finger wave and pointed to the empty seat. The others were already there, and I sat next to Karen and smiled.

"Sorry, I'm late. Traffic."

Not a lie, but I had been running a little bit late

because getting out of Tanner's hold when we had been doing the one thing we were good at hadn't been easy.

Tanner had a seminar later today. Plus, he wanted to do some things around the house, grumbling about maintenance people and repairs. And then he had to work. I wouldn't see him for the rest of the day, and I had to ignore the little pang in my heart that told me I would miss him. I had just been with him. I had plans with my roommates later, as well as a paper to look over. Tomorrow, I had hours of community service through my charity work, and I would be busy for most of the day. I likely wouldn't see Tanner at all. And that should be fine.

We had a co-parenting plan, not a relationship one.

Why then did it bother me?

"You're looking good," Victoria said as she grinned. "We ordered you a mimosa."

First hurdle. "Thank you. I have a lot of work to do, so I thought I might go with sparkling cider today. And maybe just orange juice."

"You're turning down a mimosa? What? Are you pregnant?" Janice asked, laughing at her joke.

I rolled my eyes and grinned, sipping my water.

Victoria narrowed her eyes and dropped her phone. The fact that Victoria would willingly put her cell on the table spoke volumes. "Oh my God, you're pregnant."

We were in a secluded part of the restaurant where nobody could hear us, but I winced at the sound of her voice anyway. "Please don't yell that so loudly."

"It's true?" Samantha and Charli said at the same time and then looked at each other, their eyes wide.

Janice blinked. "I thought, of all of us, I would be the one who got pregnant first. I mean, you're Natalie. When was the last time you went on a date that wasn't with one of your dad's friends?" she muttered, and the other girls tittered while staring at me.

My stomach roiled, but I tried to ignore it. Were these the women I had once hung out with for hours at a time? I had grown up with them. Had I *been* one of them?

No, that couldn't be. Maybe they had changed. Or I had. I didn't know. All I knew was that I wanted to go home.

I shouldn't have even come to this, but I couldn't say no when it came to memories. Plus, I hadn't been thinking straight lately, and given that I was finally—hopefully—through with the morning sickness, I'd thought maybe coming out to this would be a final hurrah before my life changed forever.

I could see now that coming here had been a mistake.

"Who's it with?" Karen asked, whispering. "I mean, you're not engaged, right? I don't see a ring."

"Of course, she's not engaged. We would've heard about it in the papers." Samantha shook her head. "Your mother is going to have a conniption."

Karen snorted. "We all know that she doesn't know. Because if she did, she would have told our mothers. That's how things get started."

"I'm going to tell them soon," I said, my voice firm. "I have dinner with them next week. That's when I plan to tell them. Yes, I'm pregnant. And, yes, I'm keeping the baby. Yes, I have a plan."

"I can't believe you're pregnant," Victoria muttered, shaking her head.

"I can't believe you finally opened your legs for someone," Karen mumbled, sipping the rest of her champagne. She snapped her fingers at the waiter and dinged the glass. "Excuse me. More. You know your job."

I blushed and groaned. "Karen."

"Don't do that. Just because I have the name of every little bitch out there doesn't mean I'm a bitch. Right?" She pointed at the waiter's nametag. "Right, Jeff? I'm not a bitch."

The man smiled softly, poured more champagne for everybody—including me, even though I hadn't asked for any—and walked away.

"We see he didn't answer." Samantha snorted.

"Oh, fuck you. Don't harp on me. Let's talk about this one." She pointed at me. "Natalie is finally letting loose and is now knocked up. Look at you. I thought you'd go out and want to get married and have kids and have a real career. Now what? Who's the father? Anyone in our circles? It better be. Because if it's not, your mother's going to kill you."

They all started talking at once, going through guys from our school—half of them I remembered as assholes, the other half I didn't remember at all.

I just shook my head and set down my napkin, my champagne untouched. "It's no one you know. But we're working on it. We have a plan. Please don't tell anyone. I need to be the one to tell my mother."

Janice snapped her fingers once, and everyone quieted. She narrowed her eyes and nodded. "You may not feel like you're one of us anymore, and maybe that was always the case. You always thought you were too good for us."

Pain sliced through me, and I opened my mouth to speak, to deny everything she'd just said, but Janice held up her hand.

"It doesn't matter. We all grow up and find our paths. You've clearly found yours. And, no, we're not going to tell a soul. You know the rules of our group. You may want to leave, and you're more than welcome to—you already did when you decided to go to that college of yours. But we won't tell. We won't break our code. Your mother will find out from you, and you'll have to deal with the consequences, just like you seemingly are now. We won't have anything to do with it. Congratulations on the baby. When you want a baby shower, come to us. Because I don't think your new friends can handle it."

They all stared at me, and I grew cold, wondering why in the hell I had thought coming out today was a good idea. I stood shakily and smiled. "Thank you so much for keeping our code. I'm sorry for bothering you today."

"No worries. This will be great gossip fodder whenever you tell your parents," Victoria chided.

"Of course. Anyway, I should head out. I don't want to dim your party as the non-drinking one."

"I guess we would always have a designated driver if you were around while pregnant," Samantha said as she chugged the rest of her champagne.

It seemed this was going to be a liquid brunch. I felt bad for the waiter.

I left a tip on the table even though I hadn't touched anything but my water, waved at the other girls who didn't bother to wave back, and walked away, leaving that part of my life behind.

They were all planning the rest of their lives. But

that would include luncheons and charities and nannies and everything I had growing up.

That wasn't who I was anymore.

At least, that's what I thought. I wasn't one of them. Maybe I never had been. But I wasn't sure who I was supposed to be now, either.

I drove back home in silence, annoyed with myself for going at all. Saying yes had been an automatic response, but I regretted it.

I knew they wouldn't tell anybody about the pregnancy, but my entire former world would know just as soon as my mother heard the truth.

Natalie Blake got pregnant out of wedlock by a man not of their circles.

I hated that they would look down on Tanner.

I didn't. I never had. Only they *would*. The girls and the others in my circle of former friends would make him feel like crap, and it would be my fault. Those were the people I had once been a part of. The circles I had grown up in.

I might have tried to find a new Natalie and all of that, but was that the case?

Had I changed?

Here I was, keeping secrets from my family, Tanner, and myself.

"Get in here," Nessa said from the doorway as I looked up from where I stood beside my car.

"What?"

Nessa smiled softly. "Get in here. You're back early, but we figured you wouldn't want to stay long with those girls. Come on."

I sighed, relief flooding me. I picked up my bag and walked inside, toeing off my heels as I did.

"You know you look sexy as hell in those high heels, but they also look painful," Nessa said as she hugged me tightly, kissing my cheek. I hugged her back.

"I can't believe they used to be my friends," I whispered.

"They weren't friendly those few times we met them, that's for sure," Elise said and winced. "Sorry, it's the truth."

"No, they're far bitchier than I ever remember them being," I grumbled as I sat on the edge of the couch. "And I'm hungry. I'm always hungry, and I didn't eat anything."

"We made food," Mackenzie said as she brought out finger sandwiches and other high tea cakes and appetizers.

Tears filled my eyes, and Elise cursed before holding me close. "We wanted to make you happy."

"You knew I'd be back early?"

"We knew you would probably be hungry because brunches with those women usually involve a lot of alcohol. And you always gripe that you're hungry."

"Really?" I sighed at Nessa's words. "Why didn't you remind me that I hate them?"

Mackenzie sighed and tapped my knee. "You don't hate them. You might now, after whatever happened today, but you didn't before. They are your past. We're your now. That baby is your future. And we're going to be the best aunties and uncles. We're here for you. We promise we'll help you."

"What am I doing?" I asked, looking down at my hands. "I have no idea what I'm doing. These past couple of months flew by, and we keep saying that we have our futures intact. But those are the futures of an adult, not a *pregnant* adult." I kept rambling, my voice getting higher-pitched.

Nessa made me a little plate. "Quick, eat."

"Thank you," I whispered as I bit into a peanut butter and jelly sandwich.

"We have some more upscale sandwiches, too," Elise added dryly. "But we wanted peanut butter and jelly. You can't go wrong with PB&J."

"You really can't," I agreed as I devoured it. I sipped the water they handed me and sighed. "What am I doing with Tanner, you guys? We just fell into each other. And we're not talking—at least not about the important stuff—and I have no idea what I'm doing."

The girls looked at each other and nodded in unison.

"We figured that's what was going on," Mackenzie said softly. "That sort of happened with us, too. We all fell into what we were doing, and then things imploded."

"I don't want things to implode. I want them to work out. But what does that even mean or look like? I feel like everybody's moving on and finding their paths, yet mine is being paved for me."

"That's how I felt last semester," Nessa added softly.

"And how Mackenzie and I both felt last year." Elise nodded.

"You're right. I'm being selfish. I'm not the center of the universe. I'm so sorry." I wiped away tears, and Nessa sighed and took away my plate. "Hey," I stated. "I was still eating that."

"Your pity party is done. We love you. And you *do* have plans—we've all helped you with those plans. But all of that was about that sweet baby of yours and school. Now, we'll help you with Tanner."

I looked between the three of them, my eyes wide. "What do you mean by that?"

"We'll be your sounding boards," Elise announced.

"We'll tie him to a chair and interrogate him until he comes up with feelings if we have to. I don't know." We all looked at Elise, and she blushed. "What? It seemed like a good idea."

"Let's table that for later," Mackenzie stated, her voice stoic even though her eyes were bright with laughter. "I'm sure Miles, Pacey, and Dillon can tie him down, though."

This time, Nessa blushed bright red, and my eyes widened as I looked at Elise and Mackenzie. The other girls giggled, and I joined in.

"Anyway," Nessa said, "we'll help. We've got you. You're not alone."

"Seriously, we'll always be here for you. Promise," Elise whispered.

They'd said that I wasn't alone. And I wanted to believe that. And yet, as I had seen with my other friends, people grew up and grew apart.

We would all change. And as I thought about the path in front of me, and the girls at my side, it felt as if my forever seemed far different than the others'.

And I didn't know what I was supposed to do about that.

TWELVE

Tanner

"You doing okay?" Dillon asked. I looked up at him and nodded.

"I'm doing fine," I said as I pulled a beer out of the fridge. We were in the kitchen, the others all out in the living room as we ate appetizers and got ready for dinner. The eight of us had decided to do a big group meal since none of us worked that night and had time off.

It was nice to schedule time like this, and I enjoyed it, even if things were still awkward. The group had all apologized to me more than once for how they reacted when they heard about the pregnancy. And, frankly, I still didn't blame them. It was a shock, and they should be upset with me. I was still angry with myself. I had changed the course of Natalie's life, and it was my fault. I shouldn't have wanted her as I did, and yet I couldn't change things. We couldn't go back to us not having slept together.

The fact that we were *still* sleeping together notwithstanding.

"I am sorry for how I reacted," Dillon said, looking down at his beer.

It was a craft brew and one of Dillon's brother's favorites. They served it at the bar, and Dillon had brought a case to the house. It was just a thoughtful thing to do—something Dillon did often. That was just who the guy was. He thought about us, cared about us, and always made sure we knew that.

There was no way I could ever be angry about how they'd reacted when they heard. Not with how they treated me every other day. They were good people, and I knew that. I just hoped they reminded themselves of it.

"I wasn't angry at you guys when you said it."

Dillon raised a brow. "You stormed off."

I shrugged and took a sip of my beer. "I needed to think about what the fuck I had done. Natalie and I are going to have a kid. And while we say we're making plans and figuring out our roles, we aren't. We suck at this."

"Do you want to talk about it?"

I looked over my shoulder and heard the others talking and laughing in the other room. "Maybe not right now."

"You've got it," he said after a moment. "But I'm here if you need me."

"Thanks," I whispered.

"Natalie wasn't expecting this, and I wasn't expecting her. We'll find a way to make this work. Yet, sometimes, I feel like all I'm doing is making mistake after mistake." I hadn't meant to say the words, especially after I'd just told him I didn't want to talk about it, and Dillon gave me a soft smile.

"That's how I feel every day with Elise, just lucky that she stays with me."

"You're a good man, Dillon. Of course, she stays with you."

"I don't feel like that's always the case, though. We all make mistakes. We're human. You're going to be a dad. Damn, that's just so crazy. I mean, my brothers are all in the process of having kids or thinking about it, and now my friends are. I'm not even sure how this all happened."

I snorted. "If you have to ask, maybe I should be talking to Elise right now."

Dillon flipped me off. "Fuck you."

"As I said, maybe I should be talking to Elise if that's your stance right there."

He snorted and grinned.

"We're here for you guys, no matter what. You know that, right?"

I shrugged. "Thanks." Only I didn't quite believe it. As soon as the semester was over, we would all be separating and going different ways. That was the whole point. Everyone had jobs or school or internships lined up. I did, too. That meant that we would essentially be saying our goodbyes, as we moved towards the end of the semester. While some of us would remain in the state, we wouldn't be as close as we were now. It wasn't possible. Not when we were moving away from each other. They wouldn't be here when Natalie and I had to figure out exactly how to be parents. And it wasn't their fault they wouldn't be. They each had lives.

"Okay, we'd better get back in there before the others ask us what the hell we've been doing."

"That is true," I muttered. We walked into the living room, and I did my best not to worry about what would happen next.

Miles sat on the floor, Nessa behind him on the chair as she rubbed his shoulders. I raised a brow at the two, and Miles blushed. Nessa just shrugged. "He had a long day. I'm not doing anything wrong."

"I didn't realize you'd be including us in your evening activities," I teased as I sat down next to Natalie. She nudged me with her elbow.

"Be nice."

"I *am* being nice."

"Not everybody wants to be in a poly relationship like you," Nessa teased before she blushed. "Sorry."

"No worries. And as I'm not currently in a poly relationship, you don't have to worry about me inviting you."

"Good, because I think Tanner's enough for me to deal with."

Natalie blushed as she said it, and the others hooted and hollered.

"That's not what I meant."

"It might not be what you meant, but it's what you said. I'm going to take that as a compliment."

"I don't know if you should," Pacey said with a laugh.

I shook my head, ignoring them, and leaned forward to take a little spinach cup. I popped it into my mouth. The flavor exploded on my tongue, and I groaned and leaned back against the couch. Natalie snuggled into my side. It felt as if she'd been doing it all our lives. I wasn't sure how we had gotten here, acting as if we were an actual couple and not merely two people pretending we weren't keeping secrets from each other. I didn't want to focus on that, but it wasn't easy to ignore. I liked Natalie. I was falling in love with her. And I had to stop. I needed to pull myself back. Rein it in and remind myself that she wasn't my forever. Our child would connect us until the end of our days, but she wasn't mine to keep. And that was a hard pill to swallow.

"I'm going to need the recipes for these," Mackenzie said as she wiggled next to Pacey. "Seriously, Dillon. They're fantastic."

Dillon grinned. "Thanks. It's just a quick recipe. A variation on what Aiden's been using at the new restaurant."

"I can't wait to visit," Natalie said as she ran her hand over the swell of her stomach.

That gave me a little jolt, and I tried not to focus on the movement. Our kid was in there. There was no hiding it anymore. There was no pretending. Natalie was pregnant. We were going to have a child. And it was growing inside her right now, getting bigger with each passing day. It didn't feel real, and yet it was. There was no denying it anymore. But I still didn't know what the fuck I was doing.

"You guys are always welcome, though I know we're all busy with a hundred different things."

"We are, but we can still have fun."

"That is true," Dillon added. "If you want, I can see if I can make a reservation for the eight of us. The place is hopping, and large tables are a little difficult to get, but maybe we can figure it out in the middle of the week or something."

"I cannot believe your family has two restaurants now." Natalie grinned. "It feels like just yesterday I was going to the bar for the first time, loving the homey feel of it."

"The restaurant is homey, too, if a little more upscale." Elise smiled. "The food is so good, though. I feel like I gain thirty pounds just by walking through the doors." She looked at us and grinned. "Dillon's brother, Aiden, likes to feed us to our heart's content."

Natalie groaned. "That's the life. I'm always hungry."

"Do you need me to get you something?" I asked, leaning forward.

I ignored the others' cautious looks as Natalie beamed up at me. "I'm good. I think I ate half of the appetizers on this table."

"And we still have dinner to go," Pacey added.

"I'm excited." She grinned. She was so beautiful when she smiled. It just lit up a room. She had always been that way, and I had done my best not to focus on it. I liked Natalie, and that was the problem. I liked the person she was and how she treated everyone around her. I may joke and tell myself that she was a princess and too good for me, but that was only part of it. She *was* too good for me, but she didn't think that. She thought we were the same. That we knew what we were doing. Only that wasn't the case. She was brilliant, kind, and beautiful. And she would be the mother of my child. I really wasn't good enough for her—not even a little bit.

I was only kidding myself, thinking that I could be.

We moved into the dining room after a while, taking the half-eaten appetizers with us. We gorged ourselves on pasta and sauce and ate garlic bread and squash. Everything was delicious, and Natalie ate with gusto. Considering that she had been sick for the past couple of months and barely able to keep things down, I liked seeing her eat. I couldn't have too many carbs tonight because I had to work tomorrow, but I could still enjoy myself. The fact that I was still using my body to pay for school and create a savings account for the baby should worry me, but I had enough on my plate to worry about. Nobody here except for Natalie knew about my job, and though I knew I should tell them, I didn't want them to look down on me any more than they already did—or should—when it came to Natalie. I really wasn't good enough for her, and I knew it. They knew it. And I didn't need to add fuel to that fire.

Natalie gave me a strange look, and I was afraid that I had said some of that out loud.

"What?" I asked.

"You're looking all serious over there. Is something wrong?"

Everything. But I didn't say that. Instead, I smiled, leaned down, and took her lips.

"That's just so sweet," Mackenzie said as she sagged against Pacey.

I cleared my throat and looked up at her. "What?"

"You guys are good for each other. I like it. The eight of us, all paired off. It's like it was meant to be."

Everybody chattered, and I did my best not to look at Natalie. The others were meant to be. It might have taken a while for them to get there, but it made sense for them. I wasn't even sure if Natalie and I were a true couple. We hadn't talked about it or decided on anything. It had just happened. One minute we were yelling at each other, and the next, we were changing our lives forever. It honestly didn't make any sense. But here I was—a man about to be a dad.

As the others spoke, and Natalie squeezed my knee, I kissed the top of her head, and we went back to eating. I was quiet, and I knew that Natalie could likely tell that something was wrong, but she hadn't done anything. It was all me.

I wouldn't fuck up my kid's life. My dad had been a good father before he was killed, and I wanted to be that guy. I wanted to be someone who didn't run away. Who took care of his responsibilities. And so, I would be. Only I didn't know how to be a part of this kid's life. Things weren't going to work out as the others thought. We wouldn't have a massive four-couple wedding where everything was rainbows and fucking unicorns. That's not how life worked.

As soon as the bubble burst and reality set in, Natalie would leave. And I would be left behind. I knew that clear as day. My mother had pushed me out ever so casually when I got to be too much for her. When she hadn't been able to handle her new guy and me. So, I had found my own path. Natalie would realize who I was and how I wasn't much help. She'd see how I would only be a hindrance to the future she needed. And I would prepare myself for that moment.

Frankly, I was surprised that she hadn't packed up and gone to her parents already. They had the money and the clout to take care of her so she didn't have to worry about the pregnancy and our child's life.

I didn't know why she even bothered to remain at my side.

Why *was* she staying?

I didn't have the answer. And I was afraid to look too deep. So, I would do my best to be perfect for her so she didn't leave.

I just couldn't fall in love while doing so.

I looked at the others and put a smile on my face, pretending that I was fine. That I didn't have a care in the world.

That I hadn't ruined Natalie's life and wasn't waiting for the other shoe to drop.

Only I knew I was lying to myself. And worse, I knew that if Natalie looked into my eyes, she'd see the lie, too.

Thirteen

Tanner

Why was I nervous? I was having a baby with this woman, and yet I was nervous. It didn't make any sense to me. Here we were, going on our first date. Not enough when it came to the grand scheme of things. I had been neglecting Natalie. I knew that much. If I had been a better boyfriend or whatever the hell we were to one another, I probably wouldn't be so nervous when it came to taking Natalie out to dinner.

I smoothed my hands over my shirt and frowned.

"Why is it so hard to figure out what to wear?" I growled at the mirror.

Miles snorted from my side. "Because it's spring in Colorado. It could snow later, or it could rain, or be a hundred degrees. You never know. But you're wearing a Henley. We all know that women dig guys in Henleys."

I met Miles' gaze in the mirror. "Isn't that something I taught *you*?" I asked, a little annoyed with myself.

Miles just smirked. "Yep. And you obviously did a good job, considering that I have Nessa, and you're the one who's stressed out about going on a date with the mother of your child."

That sentence kicked me in the gut like it did every time someone mentioned it. I was going to be a dad. It didn't make any sense.

"Get that panic out of your eyes."

I blinked, looking at my friend. "Why did you think I was panicking?"

"Because I know you. Total panic."

"Thank you for that. I want to throw up."

"You're fine."

"I guess I am. I should have been taking her out before this."

"You guys see each other practically every day

between school, work, and coming over here. It's not like you had time to date."

"I had time to get her pregnant," I mumbled.

Miles sighed. "True, but I hear that doesn't take that long."

I glared at the other guy. "Excuse me?"

"I'm not talking about your prowess, oh mighty Tanner. All I meant was that it doesn't take months to get pregnant sometimes. It only takes the once."

"I'm well aware, considering I'm going to be a dad soon. I can't believe I just said that."

"You're getting used to it."

"Am I? Or am I falling into a sense of despair in a new dimension?"

"Look at you, sounding like the geeky one."

I flipped him off. "Does this work, though?" I held up my arms, looking down at my dark jeans, boots, and charcoal gray Henley. I hadn't shaved in a couple of weeks, and my beard was coming in, but I figured I looked okay. I didn't look as if I just rolled out of bed, at least. That had to count for something. Although Natalie liked how I looked just getting out of bed. I pushed those thoughts from my mind. We were not going to have sex tonight. I'd promised myself that we would go on a nice date, and I would show her that I wasn't an asshole who took advantage.

So why did I feel as if I were just learning how to date?

"You look great. Are you going to that small café?"

"Thanks for recommending it."

"No worries. It's where I go with Nessa. It's inexpensive, but the food is delicious. Dillon's brother even likes it."

Considering that Dillon's brother, Aiden, had worked as a chef at a Michelin-starred restaurant, I thought that was a pretty good sign.

"Okay. I guess I can do this."

"You're not going off to the guillotine. You're taking Natalie on a date. Having dinner with her. Something you've done before. Sort of. What's different about this time?"

I shook my head. "This time, she looks pregnant, and there's no hiding it. People are going to know."

"Her classmates have already figured it out. Now strangers will, too. Who cares?"

"We're telling her parents tomorrow," I growled.

Miles winced. "So, you're worried this may be the last time you see her because she's going to be sent off to a commune?" Miles asked, and while I knew he was teasing, my stomach roiled.

"Don't even fucking tease about that."

He held up both hands. "I knew it was the wrong thing to say as soon as I did. I'm sorry. I don't know

Natalie's parents, but I know that the girls have been stressing over it. I'm here if you need me. I promise."

"I know, thanks."

"You look great. Really. I'd do you."

"You say the sweetest things, Miles."

"I try, but only for you. Now, go out, have some fun, and don't stress about tomorrow. We'll all be in our new jobs and houses soon, and you're going to have a screaming infant. Take this time of peace while you can."

I blinked at Miles, wondering where the quiet, nerdy college student I had once known had gone. In his place was this teasing, confident guy. And while I liked it, it wasn't helping.

"Seriously? Seriously."

"Now you sound like you're on *Grey's Anatomy*."

"I hate when you make pop culture jokes," I grumbled and grabbed my phone, sticking it in my pocket. "I'm on my way to pick her up. We'll have fun, damn it."

"I don't know why you're telling me that. It looks like you need to tell yourself that. Maybe a little pep talk?"

"I'm honestly afraid of what your pep talk might be at this point."

"You know, you're not wrong there," he said with a grin. "Go get your girl."

"I'll try," I whispered. Because, yes, Natalie *was* my girl—albeit for only the moment.

I walked downstairs and cursed under my breath. "I thought I said I was going to pick you up?" Her brow shot up, and Pacey glared at me from the front door. "I mean, you look fucking fantastic. Now, what the fuck are you doing here?" I asked, and Pacey threw his hands up in the air and then walked into the kitchen.

Natalie rolled her eyes, and I really looked at her then. All of her. She wore a light gray wrap dress, one that complemented the color of my shirt, which I found odd since we had done that without even talking about it. The wrap dress brushed her knees, and tall heels in another gray pattern highlighted those sexy-ass calves of hers. I didn't know how she still wore those kinds of heels, and I hoped she didn't plan on wearing them for the whole pregnancy. She'd pulled her long hair over one shoulder tonight, the waves looking so tantalizing, I wanted to reach out and wrap them around my fist. Probably not the best thing to think about, but I didn't give a shit right then. I wanted her. I always wanted her. And that was the problem.

"Mackenzie was on her way over here, so I hitched a ride. They're going out tonight, too, but to Dillon's restaurant since he and Elise are there."

I swallowed hard. "I guess that makes sense."

"I texted you," she said, her hands in front of her. I sighed, pulled out my phone, and cursed. "I didn't get the alert. I'm sorry." I stepped forward, cupped the back of her head, and crushed my mouth to hers. This was what we were good at. Anything that had to do with sex, and need, and…not talking.

I used to be good at talking with humans. Not anymore. I completely lost all sense of that when I got with Natalie. Or maybe even after the first time I saw her.

"You look beautiful. Thanks for making it easy for the night. I'm glad you're here."

She looked up at me then, her kiss-swollen lips parted. "I guess that works. You look sexy, Tanner."

The word *sexy* coming from those formerly innocent lips nearly sent me over the edge. I was in a perpetual state of hardness when it came to Natalie Blake, and she only had herself to blame.

"Let's head out. If not, I'm going to pull that dress up over those sexy-ass hips of yours and see what you're wearing under there."

She grinned. "Well, then. Good to know this pregnancy bump hasn't changed anything."

"That's an image that'll get me through dinner."

I grinned and put my hand over her stomach. It was such an inherent gesture that I hadn't realized I was doing it until I was already there. I had touched her stomach hundreds of times at this point, both of us talking to the baby because that's what the books said to do. We were going in blind and trying to find our way through. In this moment, it felt far more intimate than anything we had done before, though. I swallowed hard and met her gaze. "Hi."

"Are you speaking to the baby or to me?"

"I think both of you."

"That works. Hi."

"Now, are *you* speaking *for* the baby?" I teased.

"I have no idea. Maybe one day I'll learn."

"Sounds like a plan to me." I leaned down and, once again, brushed my lips gently across hers. "Let's head out. We don't want to miss our reservation."

The place was small, a little run-down, but the food was excellent. They were packed, and though it wasn't a high-end restaurant, they still took reservations. I hadn't minded since we had planned this, but it still felt as if this were a far more meaningful date than it should be. If anything got too deep, it would hurt like hell once things ended.

I slid my hand along hers, brushing my fingertip across her knuckles. She smiled up at me, no words needed. She had her hand on her bump, and I wasn't even sure she was aware that she was doing it. We linked our fingers together and just stood against one another, waiting for our table to be called.

"I do love a young couple in love," an older woman said from the corner. There were only two small bench seats in the waiting area, and we had allowed an elderly couple to take one while two older women took the other. Natalie hadn't minded standing in her heels, but if we didn't get our table soon, despite having reservations, I would carry her down there. She would likely hate to be the center of attention, but she was wearing goddamn heels. That couldn't be good for her back. Was it even good for the baby?

Suddenly, the woman's words penetrated my thick skull, and I cleared my throat. I looked down at Natalie, who blushed and shrugged.

"They don't need to know everything," I whispered, and I knew I had said the wrong thing.

We weren't in love, we were only having a baby. Out of wedlock.

With no emotions other than fear and turmoil between us.

Great going, Tanner. You're a fucking idiot.

"I guess they don't know anything," she grumbled. I leaned down and kissed her again.

"Sorry."

"What should you be sorry for? We're only on a date. As co-parents."

"Natalie," I whispered.

"Let's not talk about it."

"Maybe we should." I hadn't realized I had said the words until she looked up at me and pressed her lips together.

I didn't know what to say, or what I should do. If I bared myself to her, Natalie was nice enough to stay and not hurt me. And that was the problem. Once she left, I'd break, but she would stay to protect me, because that's who she was. She would stay because she thought it was the right thing for the baby.

I couldn't let her do that. I needed her to make decisions without my feelings getting in the way.

"Tanner?" a voice said from behind us. I froze, my entire body turning to ice.

This couldn't be happening. This wasn't supposed to happen.

"Tanner?" Natalie whispered, and I squeezed her hand.

"I'm sorry," I said, the only warning I could give her. I turned as my mother looked at me, a bright smile on her face. There were dark circles under her eyes as if she had been working too much. But why was she here?

"Tanner, I didn't know you'd be here. I'm so excited to see you. It feels like it's been ages."

I still held onto Natalie as my mother hugged me, and I used my free arm to hug her back.

"Look at you, looking all spiffy. And you're on a

date. How embarrassing for me to be here and run into your girlfriend. But I can't help it. I want to meet her." Mom bounced on her toes, and though I had never mentioned Natalie, and this could have been a first date for all Mom knew, she had stars in her eyes. Always had. It was probably why she was still with Jared. And speaking of Jared, I noticed he towered behind her, glowering. Cody stood beside them, and I felt another kick to the heart. They were here for a family dinner, at the café near my place.

And they hadn't called or asked to see me.

Why did I feel immense relief that I didn't have to spend time with Jared, yet felt as if I had been kicked and thrown out because they hadn't even bothered to ask if I was free?

"Hi, I'm Natalie," Natalie said as she turned slightly, hiding part of her body behind me. I knew she had done it on purpose.

She held out her hand, and my mother gave me an odd look before reaching across us to shake. "It's so lovely to meet you. But I'm a hugger. Sorry. She turned and moved to hug Natalie, but she suddenly stopped, her eyes wide.

"Oh," my mother whispered, and I groaned.

"Mom, this is Natalie. Natalie, this is my mom, Isabella. And this is Cody, my little brother." I said as I reached out to fist bump Cody's outstretched hand. My brother gave me a broad smile but didn't move forward. After all, Jared had his hand on my little brother's shoulder, holding him back.

I wanted to rip that arm out of its socket, but I refrained. Only just.

"Tanner?" my mother asked, confusion in her tone. "Is this…? What's going on?"

Everyone was looking at us now, and the maître d' had wide eyes as if afraid we might make a scene. And knowing my family, it was possible.

I cleared my throat. "Let's get out of here and give everyone some privacy," I said, and Natalie squeezed my hand. "That sounds like a great idea. It was nice to meet all of you."

"Really? You're just going to hide your girlfriend like that? Got her all knocked up and everything. I should have known you'd be a fucking loser," Jared spat.

You could have heard a pin drop in the restaurant. I held back a growl, doing my best not to say anything. Because if I did, I'd likely punch him. I'd ruin everything and there'd be no holding anything in anymore.

I would show Natalie who I was and ruin every chance I had of mending fences with my mother.

"Jared," my mother said and pressed her lips together as the asshole glared at her.

Natalie stood frozen at my side, her hand lying protectively over our baby.

"Let's get out of here," I whispered and met Cody's gaze. "Come on."

Cody moved forward, but Jared held on tight. "Let's all talk out near the cars."

He turned then, forcibly moving Cody and my mother, and I wanted to hit the bastard for touching them, but we were in public. And Jared would press charges.

"Tanner," Mom whispered.

"Not now," I snapped.

I hated myself. I didn't want Natalie to see this, but I couldn't hold back. I couldn't do anything right.

She didn't say anything more, but she did follow me outside. I swallowed hard, wondering what the fuck we were supposed to do.

"Mom, as I said, this is Natalie." I let out a breath. "And, as you can probably guess, we're having a baby."

Natalie and I hadn't practiced what we'd say when we met with others and this came up, so we might as well get through it now. Natalie had been the one to blurt it out to our friends. Apparently, it was my turn now.

My mother's hand went to her mouth before she smiled widely. "A baby. I'm going to be a grandmother."

I smiled then as Natalie leaned into me.

"I'm sorry you're finding out this way," Natalie whispered. "We were going to tell our parents this week. Tonight was just our date before we gave everybody the news. I'm showing a lot earlier than planned."

I knew Natalie was rambling because I wasn't saying anything. I needed to say something.

"So, yes, we're having a baby."

"Knocked her up, and you're not even going to marry her? What the fuck is wrong with you, boy?"

"You're going to want to watch your tone," I said softly as Natalie squeezed my biceps. "Especially in front of my mother, my brother, and Natalie."

"Can't even call her your girlfriend? Or is she… what? Your baby's mama or whatever the fuck they call it these days? Jesus Christ, I thought your dad raised you better than that."

"Don't talk about my dad," I spat.

"You going to give it a go, son? You're just some punk kid who can't even put on a rubber. You think you can take me? Come at me."

"Tanner," Natalie whispered, and I nodded tightly.

"You're not going to get a rise out of me." I looked over at Cody. "You mind heading to the car? You safe there?"

"Don't give him orders."

"You're not our dad, so you can just shut the fuck up right now," I barked, and my mother pressed her lips together. I wasn't helping things, but Jared didn't get to talk to us this way. Only, once they left, they would be alone with him. I would be the one who started shit and didn't follow through.

Like always.

Cody went off to the car, leaving the four of us alone. They'd parked two spots over, so we could still see him, but hopefully, he wouldn't be able to hear us.

"I'm not going to respond to what you just said because we're in a public place, and I'm trying to have a date with my girl here. Yes, we're having a baby. We're going to raise our baby together, and we wanted to tell you guys together. I'm sorry it came out this way, but don't talk about my mother that way. Don't talk about Natalie that way. Don't talk about anyone in my family that way. We're having a baby. Mom, you're going to be a grandma. We'll talk soon. I love you." I took a step forward, ignoring Jared's warning gaze, and kissed Mom on the cheek. "Call me if you need me."

"She's not going to fucking need you."

"We'll see."

I turned on my heel, giving him my back, knowing that it probably wasn't the smartest thing to do. But Jared wouldn't hit me here. He was good at taunting and not following through. Jared wanted me to attack.

That way, he could kick me out of the family forever, and he would have complete control. I had to be the strong one.

I pulled Natalie with me gently so she wouldn't hurt herself in those heels, and we made our way to the truck.

"Tanner, the way he spoke..."

"Not right now," I whispered.

She pressed her lips together and nodded. We got into my truck. Jared and my mother piled into the car with Cody and sped out of there before I'd even started the engine. I let out a breath, gripping the steering wheel.

"That's my family," I said after a moment.

"Your mother seemed nice. And your brother looks just like you. But that man? He's not your family. You told me he's not your family. I just wish there was a way we could get your mother and brother out of there."

I looked at her then. "I don't know how. But you're going into the right line of work for it, aren't you?"

She bit her lip. "Eventually, yes. I'm so sorry. I wish there were something I could do right now."

She reached for me, and I flinched, ignoring the hurt in her gaze. "You shouldn't touch me. Not when you saw where I came from."

"Stop it. You don't come from that. Your dad was a hero."

"They called Jared a hero, too, for fighting over there."

"Then he came back an asshole. He probably always was an asshole."

"You call me an asshole," I whispered.

"Sometimes you act like one, but not like that. He was cruel. You're never cruel, Tanner." She leaned forward and ran her fingers through my beard. "I'm sorry. I'm sorry for what he said and what he's doing. I wish there was a way we could help your mom, and maybe there is. They know about this now." She rubbed her belly. "And even if we don't have labels for each other, we're going to be parents. You're going to protect this baby just like you're trying to protect those in your family. You're going to be a great father, Tanner."

I knew she was saying all the right words, but I couldn't see them as truth. Shame crept over me, and I tried to ignore it. Instead, Natalie leaned forward and kissed me, gripping my hand. "Let's go home. We'll pick up a burger on the way and watch a movie."

"So much for our date."

"Our date is whatever and wherever we want it to be. Plus, I just want to cuddle with you and get out of these shoes."

I snorted. "Told you the shoes were a mistake."

"That's not what you said the last time when I had them wrapped around your neck," she teased, and I groaned, knowing she was joking just to lighten the mood. But it wasn't going to work completely.

She had seen the truth of who I was. Had seen where I came from.

Now, she would leave. I wouldn't be able to keep her.

Fourteen

Natalie

Why was I so nervous? Oh, right. Because I was bringing Tanner to my parents'. It was a scheduled dinner with my family, and I had told them that I was bringing someone. My mother had been so intrigued and delighted that I didn't have the heart to tell her that I would crush her dreams by not bringing someone she would approve of. I hated that I could guess what would happen with Tanner, and I knew I needed to protect him no matter what. I kept telling myself that I loved my parents, but I knew they would not be kind to him. I didn't even know if they would be kind to me.

After all, they were about to find out that they were going to be grandparents. This wasn't what they wanted for me. I knew that much. But it was what was happening. And as I felt my body change, felt Tanner next to me every step of the way, I thought perhaps this might be what I wanted. Maybe not in the sense that I'd planned it, but I wanted it now, and I didn't want to let it go.

"Are you ready?" Tanner asked as we pulled up to my parents' neighborhood. We'd taken my car as I had the gate code already keyed in, but I had let Tanner drive. He was calmer than I was at the moment, but I figured it had to be a façade. He was good at pretending when he needed to.

Just thinking about how he had tried to defend his mother, to protect her hurt. Especially because he hadn't been able to. Yet he had done his best to push all of that off and pretend that he was fine and not breaking inside.

It was so hard to find the man beneath the mask at times, but I wanted to uncover him. I just hoped it didn't destroy us both in the end.

"Natalie?"

I shook my head and reached out to squeeze his knee. He raised a brow, and I blushed. Every time I did that, he gave me a look that told me exactly what he thought about it. After all, I was a little too close to certain parts of him, and it made both of us swoon a bit. Okay, so I swooned, and he groaned, but I still counted that as somewhat of a win.

"It's just around here," I said, pointing down the street, and he gave me a look. "You put it in your GPS. I know. We're going to be okay."

"You say that, and yet I don't know. You haven't met my parents."

"You met my mother and Jared yesterday. I think we are both quite aware that I don't have the best track record when it comes to family."

"I'm sorry," I whispered.

"Don't be. It's life. You already told me that your parents might freak the fuck out, and I am prepared to stand with you. I've got you."

I looked up at him and swallowed hard. "You do. Okay. We can do this." I looked down at my stomach and grimaced. "This dress pretty much covers the bump, so at least that's good."

"Your mom's going to know, though. You can't hide it that well."

"I don't understand how some women can hide their pregnancies with clothing for so long. I seemed to pop out overnight, and there was no more hiding it."

"All you have is a stomach. You haven't gained any

other weight anywhere else. If you face forward, you can't even tell. It's only when you turn to the side that you're suddenly like, wait, there's a bump there."

I snorted. "I don't know if that's quite accurate, but I don't think I can stand perpendicular to my mother for the entire evening."

"Look at you, using the big words."

I rolled my eyes. "You're going to be an architect. I'm pretty sure you know what the word perpendicular means."

"True. But, sometimes, I'm just a poor boy from the wrong side of the tracks, who doesn't know what these big words are."

"Shut up," I said with a laugh as I shoved his shoulder. He scowled at me. "I'm driving, thank you very much. We're not going to hurt little bean over there."

I snorted. "Little bean?"

"What? I needed a name. And since we don't know the sex of the baby yet, we're going to go with *little bean*."

"Little bean. I like it. I wonder if we should keep it for the true name."

"Only for a middle name."

"Let me guess, Pinto, Kidney, or Garbanzo should be their first name?"

"Little Kidney Bean Blake."

We pulled into the driveway, and I frowned. "What about Blake-Hagen? Or Hagen-Blake?"

He let out a breath and turned off the engine. "I'm good with anything, Natalie. Just know that I'm not going anywhere."

"Tanner..." I began but knew this wasn't the time for that conversation.

I let out a breath and looked at the large and foreboding home in front of me. "Let's go."

"This place is huge," he said and shook his head. "The architecture? Fucking beautiful."

I grinned. "I lived here all my life. I love the place. As I love the place we have over in the Hamptons, and the mountain lodge, and the beach house."

He just blinked at me. "Sorry, I'm rambling and sounding like an utter spoiled rich girl."

"No. Well, maybe a little. I have a feeling we're not going to be invited to those places to look at the architecture, so you'll have to send some photos to me. Possibly through a Ouija board because your father might kill me tonight."

"I'd be more afraid of my mother," I said with a wince, and he grimaced.

"Good to know." He squeezed my hand and met my gaze. "Let's do this."

"Okay."

I got out of the car and walked around to the front where Tanner met me, his hand out.

I tangled my fingers with his, and we made our way to the door. Tanner was in black slacks and a gray button-up. He looked beautiful and as if he had been born in dress clothes, and I knew he had borrowed the outfit from Pacey. Not that Tanner didn't have nice clothes, but Pacey's were a little more high-end, and I hated that Tanner felt any shame for who he was and what he had.

I hadn't mentioned it, and neither had he, but I recognized the clothes. I hated that he felt he had to change for my family. He didn't have to change for me. I hoped he realized that.

We rang the doorbell, and Ronald, our butler, opened the door, his nod regal. "Miss Blake. Sir."

Tanner gave me a look, and then I remembered that I hadn't told him we had a butler.

"Hello, Ronald. Are they in the drawing room?"

"Yes, with cocktails. May I take your bag?"

"Thank you."

I let out a breath as we passed Ronald, and Tanner gave me another look.

"He's not always here for family nights, but it seems Mom wanted to impress." Or intimidate, but I didn't say that. However, from the look in Tanner's eyes, he knew.

This would not end well.

We made our way into the drawing room where my parents stood by the fireplace, both of them laughing at something. They looked so happy, and I knew they loved each other. They got along and were made for one another. They just had set ideals for who *I* needed to be, and that was someone settled with a person of their circle. That wasn't me, though. And while I knew that some of my friends had gone through similar things—namely Elise—my parents were just on the edge of brittle. They wouldn't approve of this, and I probably should've done it by text or telegram. But they had raised me better than that. I would tell them in person, and then I would run away.

"Mother, Father, this is Tanner Hagen."

Both my parents stopped what they were doing and looked over, slight smiles on their faces. There was some kindness there, but both gave Tanner assessing once-overs as if he were a prime piece of beef.

He was gorgeous in his attire, and he was beautiful out of it, but my parents were looking for signs of weakness.

They hadn't approved of Tanner ahead of time, so now they would scrutinize.

They introduced themselves—my dad's look penetrating, my mother's cool. Tanner shook their hands and gave them each a tight nod, all the while standing by my side. We were all silent for a moment, and I swallowed hard, awkwardness settling over us.

"Thank you for inviting us to dinner."

"I'm just so happy that you finally brought someone." My mother gave Tanner a small smile. "After all, we've been trying to help her find happiness; setting her up with a few of our friends and people in our close circles. And here she is, bringing you out of the woodwork. Yet we don't seem to know you. Do we know your family, Tanner? Or are you only here visiting? We'd love to know more."

"Mom, we haven't even had a drink yet."

"Of course, of course. What can I get you? A beer?" Mom said. And, right then, I knew we were already going downhill.

"I'm fine with water. I'm driving."

"I assume tap water, then," Mother said as she snapped her fingers. She reminded me so much of the girls at brunch that I nearly staggered back.

A maid came in with a single glass on a tray, tap water with no ice. My mother had planned this. Oh, no, this would not go well at all. And she hadn't even looked me over yet to see that I was pregnant.

I wanted to run, to spirit Tanner away and save him. I could deal with my parents, but I hated that I was essentially throwing him to the wolves.

"Mom," I said.

"What? He asked for water. And look at us. We have it."

"Thank you," Tanner said, not a single hint of his emotions in his tone. He didn't sound angry, but I *could* hear the resignation. I didn't think my parents could, though.

"So polite. I didn't think they would teach you that at that school of yours. No, not the school my daughter attends, of course. But your high school. Clemens High? Or perhaps the middle school, Clark."

I blinked, and my mother smiled as if she were the cat who ate the canary.

"Of course, we looked him up," my father said, shaking his head. "Our daughter wants to bring home a boy? We uncover everything."

Not *everything*, because they still hadn't looked down, and I knew they didn't know about Tanner's job. If they did, there would've been sharper tones right away.

No, this was because of his family. I hated this. I had done this. I had put him in this situation, and I needed to stop this from going further.

"No, we're not doing this. We are not these people."

"We're exactly these people, dear. Tanner's the one who's not like us. Do you think you can just bring home some boy you find who only wants our money? No. This is not happening."

"I don't need any of Natalie's money," Tanner put in.

"Was I speaking to you?" my mother asked, and I moved forward, trying to put myself in front of Tanner, but he held me back.

"No, but you were speaking *about* me, and I don't do that. Natalie, though? She's too kind to say what she really thinks."

I wanted to crawl under a rock, but I wasn't about to let Tanner do this alone.

"You're going to let him talk to us like that?"

"I'm going to let him do whatever he wants. He's an adult, and you're treating him like crap. Did you know his dad died in Afghanistan? That he was fighting for our country? No, you likely don't know any of that. Or maybe you do and just ignored it because all you do is say you support the troops while sneering at them. Tanner is a fantastic person, and I hate that you'll never know that."

"Of course, we're not going to know that because you won't be seeing him again."

I laughed—outright laughed. "I don't think you have a choice in that."

"We're your parents. Of course, we have a say."

And then my mother froze, her face going pale, and I knew. "No," she snapped.

I put my hand over my stomach and raised my chin. Tanner's hand was still on my hip, keeping me steady.

"Mother, Father. Tanner and I have something to tell you."

My mother snarled and threw her martini across the room. I flinched at the sound of the glass shattering, and Tanner pulled me closer, checking me for wounds.

"Are you okay?" he asked, his gaze raking over me.

I nodded. "I'm fine. Let's go."

"Don't you dare," my mother said as she gripped my wrist.

I looked down at where she held me, glaring at the tight hold where my skin was already whitening.

"Let go."

"You're going to want to let go of her now," Tanner whispered, his voice low and dangerous-sounding.

This was going far worse than I had ever thought.

"You bitch," my mother snapped, and my eyes widened, ice sliding over me.

"Let go," I hissed. My mom finally did before she started to pace. My dad came over to me and held up his hand. I flinched, but then Tanner was there, standing in front of me as he put his body between my father and me.

"You're going to want to stop that. You come at her, you'll have to deal with me."

"Tanner," I whispered, mortified. "Let's just go."

"Get the fuck out of my house," Dad snarled. "Both of you. I'll sue you. I'll put you in jail for daring to touch my baby girl."

"It's worse than that," my mother snapped as she moved forward, facing us both. "We are not having one of *his* children in this family. You know what to do. We can call Dr. Jasper right away."

Bile filled my throat, and I staggered back, only Tanner's hold keeping me steady.

"What are you saying?" I whispered.

"You know exactly what I'm saying. It's still early enough. You can end this before you make the worst mistake of your life."

"Fuck you," I whispered, and both of my parents froze, shocked expressions on their faces as if they had never heard me curse before in my life.

My mother snarled. "What the hell has this boy been teaching you?"

"You just cursed at *me*. You just told me to abort my baby. No. Fuck you both."

"Then get out," my mother snapped.

"Out," Dad agreed. "It's over."

I raised my chin. "Fine."

"And don't think you can come for our money," Mother snapped, looking at both of us.

"I never needed your money," I whispered. "Grandfather and Grandmother always took care of me. As did my aunt. And I'm going to have my own job and will have my trust funds. I don't need you."

"We'll do what we have to do for your trust fund," Dad whispered.

"You can't touch it," I said calmly, even though I was anything but.

I raised my chin and turned. "Let's go."

"I'm all for that," Tanner mumbled, and we practically ran out of the house. I grabbed my bag from Ronald, ignoring his penetrating stare because I didn't want to know what he thought.

I didn't want to know what anyone thought. We got in the car and left, my entire body shaking.

"I'm sorry," I whispered.

"Don't be. That wasn't on you."

"It's where I came from, though."

"Didn't you just say yesterday that I'm not who my family is?"

"I can't believe this."

"Honestly, it went better than I expected," he said as we pulled out of the neighborhood.

I looked at him then and blinked. "That was better than you expected?"

"I wasn't arrested. I mean, it could still happen once I get to the house, but they didn't murder me. I'm going to count that as a win."

I took in the tight line of his jaw, and I knew he was angry.

This was all my fault. I shouldn't have brought him. I should've dealt with it alone.

When the tears fell, he pulled over to the side of the road and tugged me onto his lap. He held me as I sobbed and mourned the family I thought I'd had. One that wasn't mine—at least, not anymore. And I held onto Tanner.

I would figure out things for my future. I had a job, I would have a degree, and I would be a mom.

And, somehow, I would do it all with Tanner.

I just had to hope that he didn't leave before everything changed.

Fifteen

Tanner

My hips moved to the beat, and I winked at the person in front of me before I strolled down the stage, finishing up my routine.

I enjoyed dancing, but this wasn't my favorite thing to do in the world. However, it made me enough money to pay for school, to give back a bit to my mother, and to save for the future.

The fact that this final dance would go to my child's college fund made me feel a little weird, but I didn't care. I was making money, and I was using my body to do it. Screw what anybody thought.

The pace picked up, and I went down, focusing on my floor work before I stood and did the final reveal. People screamed and giggled, and I just winked, giving them my patented grin. It wasn't the one I gave Natalie or anyone outside of this place. No, any wink or dance I gave Natalie was only for her.

I licked my lips, winked, and bowed while gathering my clothes that I could reach before heading off stage. People whistled and hollered, and I knew I'd made decent money tonight. I was still making tips, but I was also on salary because the place wasn't some run-down hole in the wall. I even got benefits, which I couldn't say about any other job I might have gotten outside of a certain coffee shop.

And they hadn't been hiring when I went to apply.

I shook my head and went back to the locker room to wash off and get ready to head home. I had a late dinner with the guys tonight. Natalie had said that she would come over later just because she wanted to.

I didn't mind in the least.

I wasn't the closing act tonight like usual, so it wasn't too late. I just wanted to get home and start the next phase of my life.

When I walked in, JC was at his locker, finishing getting ready. He opened his arms. I rolled my eyes, feeling a bit odd that I was still in my booty shorts, and he only wore a G-string, but I gave him a big hug and slapped him on the back anyway.

"Nothing homoerotic about this." He winked, and I snorted, shaking my head as the rest of the guys came in to smack me on the back, as well.

"Looking hot out there, Hagen," one of the guys called out.

"I always knew you could shake what your mama gave you. The girls are going to miss you."

"And the guys. And everybody else. You were our headliner. They're going to wonder where the hell you went."

Everyone kept talking, and I grinned, quickly getting ready to head home. "You guys have been great, but I'm out for now. My internship's starting before the semester is over, and I have to be done."

"This just means I can take your spot," one of the other guys said, pulling back his blond hair. He looked as if he could bench press me with one pinky, and he made good money for the club.

"I'll always think of you guys," I said dryly, and someone threw a clean pair of shorts at me.

"Just come back and visit. But this time, you'll have to pay to play."

"That's an image I'll never get out of my head," I added dryly.

They all started laughing and then went back to

whatever they had been doing because it *was* a workday, and there was no rest for the wicked—even those who shook their hips for rounds of tips.

"I'm proud of you," JC said after a moment, zipping his leather pants.

"For dancing?" I asked as I pulled on my regular jeans.

"That, too. You're damn good at it, and you learned a few new moves."

"I'd say you taught me everything I know, but then we'd be creeping into weird territory."

"Truth. You did good. And you never treated yourself like shit for this job. You're a good guy. I can't wait to see where you go from here."

"That means you're not just going to bounce on me now that I'm no longer employed here?"

"Never, kid. You're stuck with me."

"I like the sound of that," I said after a moment, grinning.

"Good. 'Cause you're not getting another choice. Go make bank at your new job, raise that baby, tell your friends what the fuck you did here so it's not a secret, and marry that girl."

I blinked at him, pulling my shirt over my head. "That was a lot in one sentence."

"Don't have enough time to say it all if I take my time."

I shook my head as I grabbed my bag. "You're my friend. We'll still go out for a drink or dinner whenever you want."

"Good, 'cause I want to see that little baby of yours growing up. And I want to meet their mom. You tell that girl you love her yet?"

"It's a little more complicated than that," I whispered.

"Love is always complicated. That's the whole point. You should tell her. Keeping it in your head will only hurt you both."

"She doesn't feel that way about me."

He guffawed. Literally let out a snort. "See, that's what's wrong with you kids today. You're so far in your head, you're afraid of what could happen."

"You're going to pull that old-man crap with me when you're about to get on the stage and strip? No. You're not such an old man."

"I feel like it some days. I'm almost done, too. And then I can enjoy retirement with my husband."

"Good, you two deserve it. And remember, I'm not in the same place with Natalie as you are with your guy."

"You're not, but you could be. All you have to do is talk to her."

I shook my head, and he gave me a slightly disappointed look before sighing and gripping my shoulder.

"Talk to me soon. Enjoy your night. Your freedom. And your new life."

"Thanks," I whispered and then headed out.

The ride home was quiet, and I was glad for the moment to think. The end of the season was coming up, and we were headed full swing into Natalie's second trimester. We were graduating soon, and everything would change even more.

I felt like I was in stasis yet freefalling all at the same time. To say it was an uncomfortable feeling would be an understatement.

I pulled into the driveway, grateful to see the front light on, and everyone's car in place. I turned off the engine, reached over and grabbed my bag, and sighed. I might as well tell them what I used to do for a living. That would take one of JC's to-do list items off the schedule.

I made my way inside.

"The prodigal son returns," Pacey drawled with a laugh as he smacked a kiss on my cheek as soon as I walked in the door.

I raised a brow. "How much have you been drinking already?"

"Not enough."

"Something wrong?" I asked, instantly on alert.

"No, just good news on the grad-school front. Full rides for Mackenzie and me."

"Fuck, yeah," I said with a grin.

"Look at us, growing and making decisions. Being adults."

I looked at my roommates and shook my head. "We've been adults for a long fucking time."

"That is true," Dillon said with a grin. "Yet, sometimes, most of our family members treat us like we're still sixteen."

"Not me," I grumbled and waved them off as they gave me a look.

"So, you're done with work, then?" Miles asked.

I nodded and set my bag next to the couch as he handed me a beer.

"You ever going to tell us what you did?" Dillon asked.

"I assumed he was just a bouncer. Was I right?" Pacey asked and then laughed. I took a swig of my beer and stared at them as they started to rattle off random occupation guesses.

"Firefighter."

"Male escort."

"Underground fighter. Though if you were, you can't talk about fight club."

"Porn star."

"Acrobat."

"Oh, you joined the circus."

I threw my head back and laughed at that one and gave them all a look.

"If anyone's going to join the circus, it's you," I told Dillon.

"Ah, fuck you. But really, this house is enough of a circus."

"Amen," Pacey cheered as he pointed his beer at me.

"Tell us."

"I was going to tell you anyway, but if you're going to get all grumpy about it, maybe I won't."

"We can just look in your bag," Miles said. "You don't usually bring that around us. Afraid we're going to see?"

"Handcuffs and dildos?" Dillon said.

"And if it was?" I asked, and he just shrugged.

"And you paid for school. You're not going to be in tremendous debt. Good for you."

I looked at all of them and shook my head.

"I worked at a club. As a stripper—a damn good one. It paid the bills."

Everyone just looked at me before Pacey grinned.

"I was close, and I'm kind of sad that you never danced for me."

"I mean, where were our lap dances?" Dillon asked.

"We would have paid well," Miles added, and I flipped them off.

"Thanks, guys, I was worried about what you'd think, and now you're just being assholes about it?"

"So what? You're a stripper. Good for you," Pacey added. "I couldn't do it, mainly because Mackenzie would skin me alive.

"Same with Elise."

"And Nessa."

Pacey narrowed his eyes. "What does Natalie think about this?"

"You think Natalie knows?" Dillon asked.

"Of course, she knows." Miles shrugged. "Right?"

"She saw me at that bachelorette party she went to."

"Well, then," Pacey said.

Dillon grinned. "No wonder the two of you can't keep your hands off each other. You have the right moves."

"Wouldn't you like to know?" I added, and they all laughed.

"Well, we know what the entertainment will be for our final party in the house."

I snorted. "Y'all can't afford me." I looked down at my friends and just smiled, knowing that this had gone far better than expected. But I shouldn't have expected anything less. My friends were good people, and they supported me no matter what. They understood.

Maybe I wasn't the asshole roommate. No, that title belonged to Sanders, and he no longer lived at the house.

When we finished dinner, I was a little drunk but not too much—more like a happy buzz—and full. Dillon knew how to cook, and since I hadn't had to help, I did the dishes.

The doorbell rang, and I grinned, knowing who it likely was.

"Look at that lovesick fool," Pacey said, shaking his head with a grin on his face. "The doorbell rings, and he's like Pavlov's dog, smiling wide just thinking about her."

I scowled. "It's just Natalie."

"There's nothing *just* about that smile."

And then the three of them left me alone, each going off to do their respective things while I went to let Natalie in.

She stood in the doorway, a small bag on her shoulder, and her hand over her belly.

"Hi."

"Hey." I let her inside, closed and locked the door behind her, and then I kissed her. I couldn't help it. It was tough to be around her and not kiss her.

That would be a problem if things changed.

We made our way upstairs, the house blessedly quiet so it felt like just the two of us.

"How did your last shift go?" she asked as she set her small bag down on the little couch in my room. She had left a few things over here since we were together more often than not, and I even had a toothbrush at her house. It still felt weird that we were suddenly in this relationship without actually talking about it, but I ignored that. This was easier. Just go with the flow. And pretend that I wasn't hyperventilating while thinking about what would happen when she left.

"It was good. I told the guys."

"You did?" she asked. "What'd they say?"

"You were right. They asked why I didn't dance for them, and that was about it."

"I guess you owe me a kiss."

I grinned, leaned forward, and brushed my lips across hers. "Good?"

"The best. I'm glad it went well with them."

"Me, too. I don't know what I would have done if I had to kick their asses."

"Like you would hurt your friends."

"I could."

"You're a much better guy than that, Tanner. And we both know it."

I shook my head. "Anyway, I didn't have to kick their asses, so all is well."

"That's always good. Considering that my best friends are your best friends' girlfriends. Things could get sticky."

"That's what happens when one house begins dating those in another."

"Speaking of houses, can we talk about something?"

I sat next to her on the couch, nodding. "Sure. Why do you sound nervous?"

"Not nervous per se, but this is something we need to talk about. Something we've been putting off."

Dread filled me, and I swallowed hard. "Okay."

"I'm not pushing you away, Tanner, I promise. I won't do that." She blurted the words and looked as if she had surprised herself by saying them.

Relief flooded me, but I tried my best not to show it. "What is it then?"

"I've been looking at houses."

"Houses."

"For us, for after we move out of here. I know you don't have a true lease with the guys' house because of Pacey and all, but our landlord will be setting up a new leasing agreement soon. And since we're not signing it, I know that some of the girls were planning on moving in here at least for the time being before we all make our next stops."

"I know. And you're welcome here. I mean, living with me. If that's what you want."

"It's what I want. And that leads to this next part. I was looking at houses because renting really isn't a thing right now. The housing market is so insane and overinflated that houses are just going up and being sold in cash deals every day."

I swallowed hard. "I've been looking into it, too. I still don't know how we walked into this place."

"Fate. And you guys have a great place, while ours is a piece of shit. But it's also a college house, near University Row, so that's what happens. Anyway, I've been looking at a few and talking to a realtor." She let out a breath. "I know this will be uncomfortable, but I can buy a few of these in cash using one of my trust funds." She held up a hand as I was about to say something. I felt like I couldn't keep up.

"I know it's ridiculous, and I know it doesn't make any sense, but if we go in with a cash offer, then we'll be sure to get it. We could also go for a mortgage with the two of us cosigning, and I would understand that, but it might be a little harder to find a place. These are just a few that I was looking up online. Hopefully, our realtor can go through it all and give us options. It would be wise to have a place where we can settle once the baby comes. That way, we're not stressed out about that while starting our new jobs and becoming new parents and just…everything that comes with being unique."

I looked down at the tablet in her hand and reached out, gripping her free one and noticing that she had started to shake. "You've been thinking about this a lot then?"

"Yes. I mean, I have to. I know we keep saying that we're going to look at things, and then it just never comes up because it's scary. We're talking about committing to live together. I know it might make more sense for us to get two separate homes and work on co-parenting that way, but wouldn't it just be easier if we lived in the same place? I can do whatever you want when it comes to a mortgage or not, but know that I can pay for this. I can use my grandparents' money. And it's ridiculous, and a whole other world that I know is kind of horrible, but it would help the baby. So, what do you think?"

I felt like I was out of step, but everything she said made sense. And she wasn't pushing me away. Out of breath, I leaned forward and brushed my lips against hers. "I'm in. I want to be with you, Natalie."

Tears filled her eyes, and she blinked them away before kissing me softly. "I want to be with you, too."

Relief slammed into me, and I did my best not to

shake. "Good. Now, let's look at these places and see what we can do. My credit is good, not great."

"I've been trying to build my credit with credit cards since I was eighteen." She winced. "It's sort of just always been on my mind to do so. And I know I'm privileged to be able to make that happen. So, we are not in the same realm as other people."

I shook my head and gripped her hand. "You don't need to rationalize these things to me. I get it. While I'm not going to say I'm comfortable with it, I will figure out how to deal with it."

"For the baby."

"For the baby." *And us.*

"We'll talk to the realtor and make a plan. Either we'll go with a mortgage or the entire thing. Either way, I can make the down payment. I know you're going to hate that, but we can talk about you paying me back if that's what you want to do. Or, we don't have to. We can scuttle that and just work on saving for college funds and property taxes and everything else that comes with being an adult. And being an adult is expensive. So, we might as well pool our resources and make it work."

"Should I say that I just did my last hip thrust on stage for our kid's college fund?" I asked dryly,

She blinked and then burst out laughing. "We will

earmark that for a college fund. And wow, we're really doing this."

I held her close and kissed her again. "We're doing this."

Without family. But we weren't kids. Far from it. We could make our own family.

I thought the feeling running through me right then might've been happiness, but I didn't know.

JC would likely tell me to talk to her. Tell her how I felt. But this was enough. Telling the guys what I had been doing these past four years, and telling Natalie that I was okay with moving in with her, that I *wanted* to move in with her, was enough for now.

I would tell her everything eventually. Tell her how I felt. Maybe.

Until then, we'd make this work.

Even if her world was so far removed from mine, it wasn't even funny. Anything for the baby. Anything for Natalie.

That was definitely what I would keep telling myself.

Sixteen

Natalie

I wasn't getting the odd looks for being pregnant in a bar that I expected, and I counted that as a win. It might be because this was Dillon's family bar, but you never knew.

"I'm glad we're doing this," Elise said as she leaned into me. I smiled up at her and grinned.

"What do you mean?"

"That we're just hanging out, it's good for us."

"We see each other often," Nessa corrected.

"We do," Elise nodded. "But when do we ever go out and hang out where we're not pretending that we don't have a thousand things on our minds that we should be focusing on instead of just being with one another?"

"That is true. We've been a little preoccupied for the past two years." Mackenzie sipped her wine. I was the designated driver for the night since I wasn't drinking. That way, the girls could have fun, and I could enjoy my virgin drinks all night. The bartender, Beckham, was this bearded hipster-looking dude who grinned at Elise as she walked in. He picked her up, spun her around the bar, and called her family.

He had been informally adopted into the Connollys, and that meant Elise was somehow connected to him. I didn't know how it all worked, but I liked the idea that everybody was family here. It was a warm place and comfortable. Most of the Connolly brothers were at the other restaurant for the night since this place worked like clockwork.

I knew the place had fallen on some hard times years ago when the brothers first gained ownership of the business, but I didn't know the whole story behind it. Now, though, it was bustling, and everything tasted amazing. Aiden might not be cooking tonight as he was at the other restaurant, but Dillon was.

I grinned at that thought, and Elise bumped my shoulder. "What are you smiling at?"

"Thinking about Dillon cooking back there."

Elise practically swooned. "Isn't he great? They have two other cooks here, and another chef at the restaurant, so Dillon didn't need to fill in tonight, but he wanted to. The schedules worked out so one of their lead chefs could take a day off to be with their child."

"It's good that they can all step in for one another."

"It is. Dillon still has two more years to finish his MBA, but then he'll be here, perhaps even opening a third business with the Connollys."

I shook my head. "They're going to take over the world."

"That's the goal," Elise said into her wine.

"And you still have another year, right?"

Elise nodded. "A year of training, and then I'm working on a paid internship, as well. I'm going to be busy, but Dillon and I are working it out. We might have even found a house in his brother's neighborhood."

I grinned. "Really? It hasn't sold yet?"

"No. It currently belongs to a family friend." She gestured towards the bar. "Beckham's wife, actually."

"Really?"

"Yes. Meadow has been renting it out but she wants to sell it. Dillon and I are seeing if we can scrape up the money to buy. My parents want to help, as do his brothers."

"Would you and Dillon take the offer?" Mackenzie asked, voice filled with concern.

"With the way the housing market is here, we might. We would pay them back and do whatever we could to make sure there was no debt between us. But renting just really isn't an option here. And we want to stay near family. We'll find a way to make it work, and we'll help the next generation. Plus, my parents are amazing right now. We're closer than ever, and they want to do this."

"That's good to hear," I said, ignoring the pain in my heart. Elise and her family had been on the outs because of many things in the past. Now, they were making things work. I had to hope that would be my family and me someday, but I didn't know. It didn't seem like that would be the case. And I hated the idea of it.

"What about you?" Elise asked as she looked across the table.

Mackenzie smiled. "It'll be no shock to you that Pacey's family also has another house closer to the Boulder campus."

I snorted. "Of course, they do."

"It's more of a mountain cabin, but it's not really a cabin because…hello, Pacey's family doesn't do anything by half-measures."

"So, you're going to be staying there?"

"While we save up for a house of our own, yes. It just makes sense while we're finishing up grad school before we have full-time, paying jobs. I don't know what we would do without them."

"Probably what Miles and I are doing," Nessa said dryly.

"I'm sorry," Mackenzie whispered.

She waved us off. "Don't be. I'm so glad that you guys have your families to help. And while Dad and Miles' parents want to help, we all have struggles. However, Miles said we could tell you. We signed a lease for a small apartment near campus."

"You did?" I beamed, relief sliding through me even as a pang of loss hit, too. We were all moving on, and it seemed like everything was going so quickly.

"Yep. We'll be moving up to the university, but we got lucky somehow. The rent isn't astronomical, and it will give us some time to save up to buy a house. The market's crazy here, but we're making it work."

I bit my lip and looked at all of them. "I can't believe we won't be living together anymore."

"I know. I was kind of excited to be Auntie Elise and living with you guys and the baby. Even though that'd be a little ridiculous with eight people in one house with a child."

"It would make babysitting an easy thing," Mackenzie added. "We're all going on to different grad schools and programs and jobs after this. Only we're not leaving each other, right?" she asked, and I shook my head.

"No, you're stuck with me forever. This baby will have aunties and uncles." I let out a shaky breath. "We're going to need family, you know?" Mackenzie handed me a linen napkin, and I dabbed my eyes. "I know it's just the hormones making me cry, and I hate it, but I am excited, even with everything changing. Tanner and I are looking at a few houses."

The girls shared a glance, and I frowned.

"Together?"

"Yes. We're looking at a few, and they're popping up everywhere at the moment, but they sell so quickly, it's a bit scary."

"But you're going into it together? As in living together?"

"Yes, that's what we decided. It'll be good for the baby."

"And what about you?" Nessa asked softly.

I gave them all a bright smile, even though it likely didn't reach my eyes. "It's what I want."

"Have you guys talked about your relationship? At all?" Elise asked.

I bit my lip. "We both said that we care for each other, and we like one another. And we want to be together. That's enough, isn't it?"

"Is it enough?" Nessa asked.

I dabbed my eyes again. "It has to be. We're having a baby. I got into a graduate program that's paid for, along with the job I'll have. It's going to take me longer to get things done, but we're going to make it work. Tanner will be working with the Montgomerys, and we're going to the same school. We'll find a way to make everything make sense. And the Montgomerys even have childcare on site."

"That's great," Elise said. "Only you haven't told Tanner how you feel."

"How am I supposed to do that? What if it scares him away? No, we're just going to stay with things the way they are. And when we're ready, we'll figure it out."

"Okay. If that's what you want to do," Mackenzie said softly.

"You guys are all in love, and it all makes sense to you, but things are different for Tanner and me. We might've started our relationship off backwards, but we're making our way through on this new path of ours. I don't want to rock the boat when everything else is already doing it. So, for now, we're just going to be together. We'll live together, raise a baby together, and then, someday, maybe I'll finally be able to tell him what I feel without worrying he may just run away in fear." I chugged the rest of my sparkling water, and all the girls leaned into me, patting my shoulders and trying to hug me.

"We love you. So, no matter what happens, we're here for you."

"Maybe you need to trust yourself and Tanner enough to open up to him."

I looked at Elise and swallowed hard. "What if he leaves? What if it's too much?" I whispered, my fear wrapping around me.

"What if it's not?" Nessa asked.

"We slept together once, and suddenly we were in a long-term relationship, raising a child. It's a lot of commitment for one afternoon of: *Why don't we*? I don't want to force him into loving me."

"I don't think he needs to be forced into caring about you," Elise whispered. "I see the way he looks at you."

"And I'm afraid to look back." I let out a shaky breath. Thankfully, the girls changed the subject, but I knew they were right. I needed to tell Tanner that I loved him. Needed to have a secure future when it came to him. Because it would be the best thing for the baby. Our child needed a secure future. I needed to make sure that we, as parents, made sure they knew we loved them, as well as each other. A relationship couldn't be based solely on what-ifs and a pregnancy out of the blue.

That's what I told myself, at least. And yet the fear of what would happen when everything changed still hurt.

I couldn't help but ask what-if?

What if he didn't love me? What if he cared, but not enough?

What would happen when I broke?

And what would happen when one or both of us had to walk away?

Seventeen

Tanner

Natalie frowned, putting her hand over her stomach.

I looked up from my computer and narrowed my eyes. "What's wrong? Is it the baby?"

She shook her head, then shrugged. "Just a kick. Actual kicks."

I lifted my arm as if to touch her stomach, then stopped. We were in this odd space where we both knew we weren't talking to one another about the important things—or at least those regarding the two of us—and I could feel the tension every time I took a breath.

I just felt as if we had fallen into this so quickly. It was almost as if we weren't the ones in charge of this, and I wanted to give her options. I didn't want to force her into anything. I wouldn't push. But, damn it, that wasn't like me. I didn't realize how much I had changed in the past year, but here I was, not able to go back.

She tilted her head and looked at me. "Do you want to feel?"

I swallowed hard and looked at my hand. "It's not hurting you?"

"Not right now. I mean, sometimes I feel a little flutter like it's going to be a bigger kick soon. Eventually, if they get your athletic skills, they may kick my bladder into submission, but I don't know if I really should be talking about my bladder with you."

I swallowed hard again as I leaned forward and set my hand on her stomach. I didn't feel anything, just her warmth. She gently tugged on my wrist and moved me to another part of her belly. I jolted as something touched me, and I pulled away, my eyes wide. "That was…that was a baby."

She smiled, her eyes filling with tears. "It's really real."

It had been real since that first test, but this just

made it more so. She had been to numerous doctor's appointments, but I had only been to the first couple. I'd had exams, my thesis advisor meeting, and a presentation for what seemed like every other class. We had done our best to try and move everything around, but with our insurance and her busy schedule, I hadn't been in the room to hear the heartbeat or anything from the doctor other than secondhand. Natalie had even recorded the meetings for me and had brought in questions, but I'd still felt disconnected. As if I weren't part of this. Only, I was. We were moving in together. We were having a baby.

And I needed to tell her that I loved her.

"Wow," I said at another kick.

"Just wait till I hit the third trimester. It won't just be these little flutters anymore. They'll be full-blown kicks. You can even see the baby moving under your skin." She shuddered. "I know I'm supposed to be okay with that, but it kind of creeps me out."

"I'm so glad you said that. Because it's always creeped me out, too." We met each other's gazes, then burst out laughing.

"Okay, then. So it's not going to freak you out too much being in the delivery room? Elise said she would be my coach for it if you don't want to be in there. You know I'd like you to be in there. As a co-parenting thing."

Every time she said *co-parenting*, my heart died a little. I knew she was protecting herself by saying it, by wanting to include me in the baby's life while not forcing me into it, and yet we just kept circling each other. I leaned forward and kissed her softly. "I want to be in the room. And I'm going to be in the room for the next appointment."

"Good. And then you can take the birthing classes with me and watch videos of babies being born, and probably never touch me again afterward."

"It's natural, right?"

"Yes, but we're going to see things. You're going to see things. And now maybe I want Elise to be in there. I can scar *her* for life and not you."

I snorted. "Husbands or, you know…partners are in the room all the time. It won't be that bad."

I had accidentally said the word *husband,* but it wasn't like I was about to propose. I didn't even have the balls to say that I loved her. Why would I say more?

"I promise, I'm still going to want you even after you birth a kid. It may scar us forever, but I'm sure you'll eventually forget it. Doesn't your body just give you hormones or something so you forget it?"

"The pain of childbirth. So you want a second one. That's what I read, or at least that's what people joke about. I don't think there's one for the dad, though."

"Dad," I repeated, shaking my head, a small smile playing on my face.

"It still feels like we're playing house sometimes, doesn't it?" she asked, her voice soft.

I nodded. "But we're figuring it out.

"We are."

I opened my mouth to say something, to tell her how I felt, but then my phone chirped with my mother's tone, and I cringed. "Sorry, that's my mom."

"Get it. I hope she's okay." Natalie frowned, rubbing her stomach, and I picked up my phone, answering the call.

"Mom? What's wrong?"

"Nothing's wrong. Can't I call you to see how you're doing?"

"Of course," I said, although she hadn't called me at all or answered my texts other than a quick one that said she was fine since the incident in the parking lot.

"What's going on? I asked.

"I was wondering if you'd like to come to dinner at the house. Bring Natalie. I'd love to get to know your girlfriend. Or, you know, the mother of your child. Cody will be there. And me."

She hadn't mentioned Jared, and I sighed. "Is Jared out of town?

"He's going fishing with his friends, so he won't be here. You won't have to worry about him."

"Mom..." I began.

"I don't have time, Tanner. You just don't know him as I do."

Or I didn't let him control me as she did. And I couldn't stop it. I couldn't do anything. I could only send money and hope to hell that she got a clue. And that Cody would be okay.

"What day are you thinking?"

"Does tomorrow work? He'll be gone for three days, and tomorrow will be a nice day for it. Unless it's too late notice."

I looked up at Natalie. "What do you think?" I asked since my mom's voice had carried.

Natalie nodded, looking down at the calendar on her phone. "Of course. What should we bring?"

"Did you hear her?" I asked.

"I did. She has such a lovely voice. And you don't have to bring anything. I'm making your favorite—ribs with potato salad and corn on the cob."

My stomach grumbled. "You know I love your barbecue sauce."

"Because I make the best. We'll see you tomorrow. Around six?"

I looked over at Natalie, and she nodded. "That'll work."

"Okay, I can't wait to see you, baby boy."

"You, too. Love you, Mom."

"Love you, Tanner."

She hung up, and I looked down at my phone. "It seems we're having dinner with my mother."

"That's good. Because our baby will need at least one sane grandparent, and we both know mine aren't it."

I leaned forward and kissed her again. "I'm sorry."

"It's not your fault. I knew my parents would react badly. I just didn't know it would be that bad. Still, it's fine. They'll come around, or they won't. I went to college, and I'm getting my degree and trying to get a job to be self-sufficient and figure out my life. I don't need to lean on them anymore. Am I upset? Yes. Will I get over it? I'll find a way, because it's not about me anymore. It's about the baby we're bringing into this world. And they don't need to be raised in hate. They need to be brought up with hope, and lo—" She cut herself off and grimaced.

"And love," I whispered.

"Yes. And love."

I met her gaze, the words I couldn't say on the tip of my tongue. Her phone rang, breaking us apart, and she sighed, looking down at it. "It's the new job."

"Answer. I'll get back to work."

One day, we would actually finish this conversation. At least, I hoped to hell we would.

. . .

We pulled up to the small home I had lived in for the last few years with my mother. They tried not to look at how shabby and run-down it was. It was nothing like the mansion that Natalie had grown up in, but it was still home—or at least it had been until Jared pretty much kicked me out.

I tried not to be self-conscious, but it was kind of difficult when comparing the two. This is where I was from. It was utterly different from where Natalie had grown up.

"I love the little flower boxes on the windows. Mom never let us do any gardening. Apparently, we weren't good at it," she said dryly as she held the flowers on her lap. "I think your mom will like these since they are the same color."

"That was just luck, not going to lie," I said softly.

"We need all the good luck."

"Yes, we do. Now, let's go eat some ribs."

"I think I could eat a whole rack by myself. I didn't realize pregnancy cravings would be this bad. I expected pickles and peanut butter. Not everything in the existence of food."

"I like you full and happy."

"You're not going to like it much when I'm asking you to go out and get ice cream at two o'clock in the morning."

"If that's what I have to do, that's what I'll do."

"You are too good to be true sometimes." She leaned over as I tangled my fingers with hers.

"We'll see."

The front door opened, and my mother stood there, a bright smile on her face. She walked out, Cody following her, and I pulled Natalie towards them, my heart fuller than it had been in a while. This was the family I wanted. The closeness that I had missed. If Jared was gone, things would make sense. Only I knew that wasn't feasible. I could hope, though.

"Mom."

"Tanner, honey. You look so good. Now why don't you reintroduce me to your girl here."

"I'm Natalie. Tanner's, um, girlfriend." I heard the *um.* I knew we all did, but *girlfriend* worked. At least it was better than co-parent.

Mom grinned, shielding the sun from her eyes with her hand. "It's so good to see you. Look at my baby boy." She rose on tiptoe and kissed me on the cheek, and then moved towards Natalie. "Hello, Natalie, I'm Isabella. It's so good to meet you officially. I'm sorry for how we met the first time."

"Let's count this as the first time. It's good to meet you, as well."

"Do you mind?" Mom asked, her hands in front of her. Natalie shook her head and reached out for my mom's hand.

"Of course, not. Here. The baby was active earlier, but they've been a little quiet now. You might be able to feel a kick, though."

"I do. Oh, wow. I'm going to be a grandma." She blinked away tears. "How am I going to be a grandma, Tanner Hagen?"

"Do you want me to explain that?" I asked dryly, and Natalie blushed.

"Tanner."

"Hey, I know how babies are born," Cody said, and I groaned.

"Sorry, kid." I shook my head, holding back a smile. "By the way, Natalie, this is my kid brother, Cody. The bane of my existence, but he's kind of cool."

"Of course, I am. It's good genes."

Natalie beamed. "It's nice to meet you both. We brought flowers," she said, handing them over as my mother blushed. "You have a lovely home."

"Thank you. I don't know what we'd do these days without Tanner helping us, but he's so much like his father. A good man."

I didn't get that familiar pang I usually did when it came to my dad, but to be compared to him? No, I wasn't like my father. I wasn't that good of a man, but I tried. I always tried.

"I'd love to hear more about him when you have

time. From either of you. Stories to tell this little one about their grandfather would be nice. You know?"

Mom gave us a watery smile. "He would have been an amazing granddad."

"Yes," I said, letting out a harsh breath. "He would have. Come on, let's get inside before a chill comes."

"It's not chilly. It's quite nice," Natalie teased. She looked over at my mom. "He's forever trying to get me to sit down and put my feet up and get out of the cold. It doesn't matter if I've been sitting for hours and just want to walk around campus or something. He has to have his way."

"That sounds about right. However, take it while you can. Soon, it's going to be all about the baby, and you may never get another foot rub."

Natalie raised her brows. "There are foot rubs involved?" She looked at Tanner. "You've been slacking."

"Apparently." I raised my hands in a what're-you-going-to-do gesture.

"Come in inside. Dinner is just about ready. I was so excited. I might have gone a little overboard."

We piled into the house, and I inhaled the sweet scent of ribs. "It smells great. Do you need me to get them off the grill?"

"No, I already did that. I didn't want to leave them

on the grill while I was outside. If you want to start dividing them up, though, you can."

"I've got that. Let me wash my hands."

I went to the kitchen and started working as if I had been doing it forever. Cody began showing Natalie around. Mom came into the kitchen with me and wrapped her arms around my waist, pressing her head to my shoulder. "She's good for you, Tanner."

"Oh, yeah?" I asked, swallowing hard.

"I'm not going to pry too much," Mom whispered, and I grinned over at her.

"Sure, Mom."

"I promise. But you look good together. I know I don't have any right to ask questions, but you seem like you're stepping up and being a good man. I can't believe I'm going to be a grandmother, and that my baby's finishing college. You're all grown up."

I kissed the top of her head and grinned. "I'm trying. I don't know what's going on between Natalie and me. Other than we're trying to be good parents. We're even looking at houses," I muttered, and Mom grinned.

"Truly growing up then. This is good. I'm so happy for you. We'll talk more over dinner. And I promise I won't pry or give Natalie the third degree. But I love her already."

"You don't even know her, Mom."

"You love her, so why shouldn't I?"

She moved over, and I swallowed hard. Apparently, my mother could tell that I loved Natalie just from a single look. Could everybody else tell? Maybe that was just Mom's wishful thinking—or her superpower.

I didn't know, but I pushed it out of my head for the moment as I set the ribs on the table, and Mom pulled out the side dishes.

Natalie walked back into the kitchen with Cody, a smile on her face. "I love your home, and the baby picture with Tanner in the baby pool with his little bare bottom up in the air was amazing."

I groaned. "Mom, I thought you threw that away," I grumbled and pulled Natalie's chair back.

Mom waved me off. "Of course, I didn't. I also made sure that the framed version of it was right in our living room."

"Mom." Heat rode high in my cheeks in the form of a blush, and Natalie just grinned at me.

"It's a cute baby butt."

"Mom never took photos of me like that," Cody said.

Mom just shrugged. "I love how cute he is in that photo. There are others where he's pulling on his penis, but there were many photos of him doing that. Little boys do that. Often."

I sputtered.

Natalie's eyes widened. "Really?"

"Oh, yes. The first thing I can tell you about raising boys is that they love their penises. They love you, and then they love their penis."

I groaned. "Please stop saying penis."

"Yes, please stop saying penis, Mom," Cody said with a laugh.

Natalie wiped tears from her eyes and shook her head. "Everything looks wonderful, Mrs. Hagen."

"Call me Isabella. Please."

"Okay, I can try. I'm not good at doing that, though."

"It's fine. When I talked to my mother-in-law, I always sputtered and felt like I didn't know how to speak, even though I used to be good at it. I'm rambling now, though. So, apparently, I've lost some of my social skills."

"You're doing great, Mom."

I grinned before ice filled my veins as I looked at the screen door when it slammed open. "Isabella, who the fuck is parked in front of the house?"

Natalie reached out and gripped my hand, and I immediately knew that tonight wouldn't go well.

Mom stood, her hands balled into tight fists in front of her. "Jared, you're home."

"Of course, I'm fucking home. Nothing's biting out there." Jared walked in and glared at us sitting at the table. "You invited that boy over without even asking? I leave, and you think you have run of the house?"

I narrowed my eyes. "It's my mother's house. And she invited me, her *son*."

"I wasn't talking to you, asshole."

"Tanner," Natalie mumbled, and I shook my head. I needed to hold myself back. If I did something rash, I'd never be able to take it back.

"Jared, please. There's enough food for everybody."

"You didn't even set me a seat? Fuck you."

"You're going to want to stop talking to my mother that way," I said, standing up slowly. Natalie pushed her chair back, covering her stomach. "We were just trying to sit here and have a nice dinner."

"I don't fucking care." He turned on my mother again. "You won't cook ribs for me usually because you say it costs too much money. And then you do it for this loser? No. I'm the man of the house. He moved out." He shot a finger in my direction. "Like he should have. Now, he's coming back and trying to suck on your teet or whatever the fuck this is. No."

My hands shook. "Watch what the hell you're saying to and about my mother."

Cody moved out of the room as if he were used to this yelling, and I knew right then and there that this needed to stop.

"You're going to need to back off. You're not on this lease. You're not part of this family. All you've done is yell and treat my mother like shit."

"You'd better get them out of my face, woman. You think you can come over here with this tramp who spread her legs for you, boy? I see that car out there. Some rich piece of shit. Some foreign job and not even American-made. I see you landed yourself a rich whore and got her pregnant. Good for you. But go make your own family, and get the fuck out of here."

"Back. Off," I growled, right in his face.

Jared was drunk. He smelled of whiskey, and I had to wonder how in the hell he had even driven here without crashing.

Natalie stepped behind me, her hand on my back. "Come on, Tanner. Let's go home."

"Look at that. She sure is sweet. Doesn't look like your mom, but maybe she feels like her." Natalie let out a squeak as Jared moved over and tried to slide his hand up her dress.

I didn't even think. I took the man's wrist, squeezed, and twisted. Jared let out a growl and punched out at me, but I was faster. I hit the man, once, twice, and then again. Jared was down, and then Natalie was tugging at me and crying.

"Jared? What the hell?" a deep voice said from the

doorway. A couple of Jared's fishing buddies came through the door, phones in hand.

"Back off him. What the hell are you doing?"

People were shouting, and I put myself in front of Natalie. Jared wiped the blood off his face and growled as one of his buddies called the cops. I shouldn't have hit him. I should have left or done something else. Anything else. Now, I had to stand here and wait for the authorities to come because the other men blocked my exit.

What the fuck had I been thinking?

When the cops finally came, I didn't resist. There was no need to. Jared's friends told them what'd happened, leaving out the fact that Jared had driven home drunk and then had assaulted Natalie.

I left my pregnant girlfriend with my crying mother and pale-as-death brother at the house with a bleeding Jared. I could only see them marginally from the back of the cop car, my arms handcuffed behind me as I wondered where the hell I had gone wrong.

Then again, this was who I was. The man I'd become. This was a place I knew I'd always end up. Natalie had seen it all. Maybe it was good that I had never told her I loved her. There was no coming back from that. Now that she had seen who I truly was, she'd walk away.

Frankly, I wouldn't blame her.

EIGHTEEN

Natalie

I waited in the police station, clasping and unclasping my hands in front of me. I had been shaking and called Dillon as soon as I got into my car. He now stood beside me, the other roommates deciding not to join us in case it was too much for Tanner once he got out—or too much for everybody standing there.

"I'd ask if you're okay, but clearly, you're not."

"He shouldn't have been the one in the back of that cop car," I whispered. "He shouldn't be here."

"I know," Dillon said.

"Jared should be here. You didn't hear the things he said. See what he did." I swallowed hard, ignoring the bile rising up the back of my throat. I could still feel Jared's hand on my leg, and I wanted to go home and shower. To forget this had ever happened. But I couldn't yet. First, I needed to deal with the rest of the evening.

I was so afraid that what had happened tonight would hurt Tanner's chances for everything he had planned for after graduation. Would the Montgomerys understand? Would his grad school?

I didn't know, but I was honestly worried.

I was so scared, and I wasn't sure what we were supposed to do now. Regardless, I would stand by his side and hope that he understood that this wasn't his fault and that I was here for him.

"We'll figure it out. All of us."

I looked up and saw Dillon's frown. "Did I say that out loud?"

"No, but I saw it on your face. Tanner is a good person. He doesn't deserve this. He's worked hard to get where he is, and one asshole isn't going to change that." He whispered the last part, and I knew it was for my benefit. There were cops all around, but everything felt all-consuming and painful.

I wasn't sure what we were supposed to do, but I knew I wanted to go home. Needed to make sure that

Tanner knew we were safe. And that I wouldn't walk away.

I should have told him how I felt. I should have told him so much. Maybe if I had, he wouldn't blame himself for everything.

I looked up as Isabella and Jared walked past, and I wanted to scream. Isabella should have stood up for her son. She should have done *something*. I hated her just a little bit right now. From the look on her face, though, it looked as if she hated herself more.

She stepped forward and pulled away from Jared when he scowled.

"I'm so sorry," she whispered.

"What's going to happen?" I asked, my voice wooden. I would not give this woman the benefit of the doubt. Would not trust her or believe her. She had let her son be whisked away in handcuffs and hadn't pleaded for him. She had merely stood there in shock. No. I couldn't like her right now, at least not until Tanner was out and safe.

"Jared isn't pressing charges." She scowled over at the man and raised her chin, making me like her a bit more. "He won't."

"Good," I exhaled, relief spreading through me. "Because I'll be pressing charges if Jared doesn't drop them against Tanner."

I met Isabella's gaze and then glared at Jared.

"Really? You think that's going to work for me?"

"Try me," I said but stopped when an officer led Tanner out. His fingertips had dark ink on them, and I wanted to scream. Wanted to shout. But there was nothing I could do. At least, not in front of these people.

The officer said a few things, but I couldn't hear what. All I could do was wait to take Tanner home so I could tell him that everything would be okay. Relief speared me at the thought that Jared wouldn't be pressing charges, but this wasn't over. Not by a long shot.

My body started shaking, and Tanner cursed under his breath. He spared a look for his mother, who leaned closer to Jared, and I had to wonder what the hell would happen with them. When she walked away, I saw the hurt in Tanner's face from where he stood in front of me. He cupped my face and leaned forward. "Breathe. You're okay."

"But what about you?"

"Let's just go home."

Home. That had to count for something. It needed to.

At least, that's what I hoped.

"Thanks for getting here. Did you drive?" Tanner met my gaze, and I nodded.

"I drove right over. The officer said they were

bringing you to the station, and I got here as quickly as possible. I called the rest of the roommates. They're all at the house. They didn't want to overwhelm you."

I felt like *I* was overwhelming him right then, so I didn't say anything else. He looked at Dillon and nodded. "Thanks for staying with her."

"I'll follow you back to the house," Dillon said, and there was no room for argument there.

I was glad that Dillon could speak because I felt as if I had too many emotions swirling in me and couldn't keep up.

We made our way to the car, and Tanner gripped my hand. I didn't know if he was using me as a lifeline or trying to say he could be mine. Either way, I leaned into him, holding onto his arm as our fingers tangled. "Let's get home. You've got to be hungry."

"I honestly don't think I could eat right now, Natalie."

"Okay. Whatever you want."

"You don't need to be nice to me."

We got in the car, and I frowned at him.

"What do you mean? I'm not nice. I'm just me."

He gave me a sad smile. "You know the truth in that statement hits home, doesn't it?" I didn't know what he meant by that, but we sat in silence as we headed home, dealt with traffic, and finally pulled into the guys' driveway.

Dillon parked beside us, and I was grateful that he didn't block me in. I didn't know if Tanner would want me to stay, and that thought hurt me.

I put my hand over my stomach, but the baby wasn't kicking. They were finally sleeping after a long day of somersaults, and I was grateful for that.

I followed Dillon inside, Tanner behind me. I looked over my shoulder. But there was nothing on his face. His expression was stony. As if he were so ashamed, he needed to hide.

"I'm glad you're here." Pacey lifted his chin as he came up to Tanner. "We were about to bake a cake with a file in it," he added, trying to alleviate the tension.

Tanner smiled, though it didn't reach his eyes. I wasn't sure what to say, but I knew this wasn't working. I wanted some time alone with him. To tell him that things would be okay. But he let go of my hand and pulled away from me.

It felt as if he had kicked me, but I didn't let it show.

He moved to the sideboard and poured himself a finger of whiskey. "Sorry to worry you guys. Everything's fine. Jared's not pressing charges."

"Is he still staying with your mom, then?" Elise asked, frowning.

"Looks like," Tanner said as he downed his drink

in one gulp. "I've got to figure out what the fuck to do about her, but especially about Cody. I don't want him anywhere near Jared."

Dread filled me, and I nodded. "I'll try to help as much as I can."

He gave me a small smile. "I don't know if there's anything we can do, but maybe we'll try. Sorry for keeping you guys up," he said as he looked at the others. "It's been a long night, and I'm finally a little hungry, but whiskey sounds better."

"We saved you some food," Mackenzie said as she stood up. "It's warming in the oven."

"Maybe I'll eat. I don't know. It's just been a shitty night, you know?"

I looked at him and then at the others. Mackenzie gestured towards the kitchen. I cleared my throat. "Come on, let's go get something to eat. Little bean and I are hungry, too."

He straightened then. "You're right. I'm sorry. You've got to be starving."

"I wasn't hungry until just now, so it's not a big deal."

"We'll give you guys some space," Elise said as she looked at the rest of the roommates. "We're here if you need us." She was looking at Tanner, but I knew she was speaking to both of us. We hadn't been in this situation before, and I just had to hope that Tanner wouldn't pull away completely. He needed us, even if he didn't think so. I wanted him to understand that.

Tanner led me to the kitchen, but he still didn't touch me. I hated feeling so far away from him, but I wasn't sure what to do.

"Dinner looks good," he said, pointing to the enchiladas. "Looks like Dillon's recipe."

"I thought you had an enchilada recipe, too," I said.

"We do. And it's fun to have competing dinner nights sometimes. But I'm glad the food's here. Sit down. I'll feed you."

"I should be feeding you. You've been through a tough night."

He frowned at me. "Not really. Just a normal one."

"Tanner, stop."

"I'm a bad bet, Natalie. You know that."

I frowned, even as ice slid over my body. "Don't say that. Jared has nothing to do with you."

"You saw where I came from. I was in fucking jail tonight, Natalie. Jared wants me to owe him something, and that's why he let me out."

"If he hadn't, I would have charged him."

"Because he fucking touched you," he growled.

"Yes, he did. He didn't hurt me because you were there. You're always there."

"Not enough," he whispered.

"Tanner."

"I need some time to think, Natalie. Let's get you fed, and then I'm going to bed. The girls can take care of you tonight."

I knew he was hurting. I knew the shame overwhelmed him. But pain sliced through me anyway, followed quickly by anger.

"You know what? I think I'm going to just eat at the house."

"Good. Give us both some time to think."

"No, I'm giving you time to breathe and to eat. And then we're going to talk tomorrow. This isn't over."

"Natalie," he began, but I cut him off.

"No. Be with the guys tonight. Do what you need to do. And then tomorrow? We're going to talk."

"Okay."

"What happened to you isn't fair. It's not fair what's going on. But you're not alone. You got me?"

"Sure."

I knew he didn't understand. I knew he wanted to keep pushing me away, but I wouldn't let him. I would give him tonight because he needed it. He needed to talk things out with the guys, and I understood that.

Tomorrow? We would figure it out.

There wasn't any other choice.

Nineteen

Natalie

I used to think I was a sensible person. That I spoke my mind, even when things were difficult. Apparently, I was wrong. Here I was, going through my final paper from one of my classes, sitting next to Tanner in my living room, and not talking about the fact that he had practically kicked me out of his home after the arrest.

It didn't matter that his mom and Jared didn't press charges, or that the Montgomerys and everyone else we talked to didn't care about what had happened because they understood that it wasn't his fault. None of that mattered because Tanner felt as if he wasn't good enough for me.

I wasn't sure how to fix that. I couldn't prove to him that I needed him. That I wanted him. It wasn't something tangible.

And it was clear he was looking for the next excuse to walk away.

I didn't want to be the one to give him that excuse.

I wasn't sure what to do, but for now, we were just sitting and working. Tanner sat next to me, frowning at his laptop, an open baby book next to him.

We were trying. Although I knew things were rocky. And I really didn't know how to fix it.

I just wished I knew how to help him.

"I'm trying to figure out this stupid problem, but at the same time, I keep looking at page ninety-seven."

I blinked and looked up at him. "What do you mean?"

"You remember page ninety-seven." He shuddered.

"Ah, yes. The infamous ninety-seven. Where it provides all the details of why you're never going to sleep with me again," I said dryly.

He frowned, took my chin, and brushed his lips against mine. "No, you're not going to want to touch *me* again after page ninety-seven."

"Oh, great. Now I'm never going to get that image out of my mind. Childbirth is beautiful."

"Whoever said that hasn't been there."

"*We* haven't been there." I put my hand over my stomach. "Little bean is getting bigger."

"Little bean has their checkup coming up."

"The doctor already knows the baby's sex. Are we going to find out?" I asked.

He met my gaze, and I so badly wanted to tell him that I loved him. I just wanted to lean forward and tell him that everything would be okay. But I knew telling him right now wouldn't be enough. It wouldn't be right. He was scared, and he needed to come to me of his own accord. I couldn't trap him with my words or my belly or the baby growing in my womb.

He needed space, and I was trying my best to give it to him.

"I think I'm up for whatever you want."

"That's a cop-out."

"We're decorating the baby's room at the house in bumblebees. That's yellow. Does it matter?"

I grinned. "Not really. We'll have multiple names picked out because we don't want to choose one until we meet the baby. So, that's one unknown. Everything else…we can get written lists and color-coordinate it all."

"That sounds like a plan," he whispered before kissing

me again. I moaned, needing him. I had thirsted for him since I had woken up that morning. Now, I wanted him more than ever. I didn't know if I could blame the hormones just then or the fact that he was Tanner.

It was hard to focus when he was around.

He leaned over me, sliding my laptop away, and I moaned again.

"The girls out?"

"Yes, but this is a common area."

"You know one of the guys has fucked his girlfriend here. I'm just saying."

"Maybe. But you and I will not be fucking on this couch."

"Okay. I guess I'll just have to carry you into the bedroom and fuck you there."

I grinned. "If that's how you're going to seduce me..."

He met my gaze, his expression turning solemn. "I'll always want you. I can promise you that. Sometimes, I can barely think with how much I want you. I didn't expect you, Natalie."

My heart shuddered, and I swallowed hard. "I didn't expect you, either."

He opened his mouth to say something, and my heart leaped into my throat. And then the doorbell rang.

I wanted to scream.

"I'll get it."

"It's my house."

"But I'm going to get the door. Your feet are up."

"Weren't we just going to do something where my feet weren't going to be up?"

"Your feet were about to be over my shoulders. So, yes, they would be up."

"Tanner," I whispered, my cheeks heating.

"Just pause on that thought," he whispered. Then he kissed me again before heading to the door. I straightened my clothes, hoping I didn't look too mussed. It was hard to stay clothed when Tanner was around. I could say one thing—we were good at that part of our relationship. Maybe nothing else, but that part we could do.

He opened the door, and I froze, seeing who stood on the other side and feeling as if I might be hallucinating.

"Ah. Tanner is it?" my father said, clearing his throat. I stood, hauling myself from the couch as my father held out his hand.

Shock slid over me, and I blinked.

My dad cleared his throat. "I'd like to start over with meeting you."

If my father had shown up in a clown costume

doing a little dance for the baby, I would've been less surprised.

"Dad?" I asked as I moved to Tanner's side. I touched his elbow, and Tanner shook himself out of whatever daze he was in before he took my dad's hand, giving it a shake. "Tanner Hagen. I'm only shaking your hand because you're trying. But after what you did last time we saw you? You're making it a little difficult for me to want to not slam this door in your face."

I looked up at him then and gave him a slight shake of the head. Tanner wanted to protect me, and I was grateful for that, but this was a moment where I needed to stand up for myself.

"What are you doing here, Dad? It's been weeks, and you haven't contacted me. You haven't texted to see how I'm doing or to talk about the baby. The last time I saw you, you tried to hit me, and then you stood there while Mom said those horrible things." My heart clutched. I looked around my father's shoulder, but Mom wasn't standing there. He had come alone.

Dad cleared his throat again. "Can I come in?"

I shook my head as Tanner took my hand. "I'm not ready for that."

My dad gave me an approving look, then did the same for Tanner before nodding. "I understand. I do. I just came here to say I'm sorry. For my actions. For what I said. I was shocked, and I shouldn't have been.

You're an adult, and you can make your own choices. You came to tell us something wonderful, and I reacted like a horrible fool. I need to work out some things, but I wanted to say I'm sorry."

Tears pricked my eyes, and Tanner squeezed my hand.

"Thank you for saying that. I honestly didn't think you'd react that way. Yes, I thought you'd be annoyed that I wasn't following your path or your dreams, but I never thought you'd try to hit me."

"I've never once hit someone in my life. And I can't believe I almost did with you. I don't know how to ask for your forgiveness, and I know you won't forget it, but I am sorry. Congratulations on the baby. And I'm with you for every choice you make. I need to work on some things with myself, but I'm here. Anything you need. I'm here."

I looked at him then. I was so confused. "Mom didn't come?" I asked, my voice low and fearful.

My dad met my gaze and stuffed his hands into his pockets. "Your mom and I are taking a break."

I staggered back, and Tanner cursed under his breath. "Okay, you need to sit down."

"I'm fine."

"No, you should sit down, Natalie," my dad added and met Tanner's gaze.

Great, now they were ganging up on me. However,

my head swam, so I let them lead me to a chair to sit down. Dad closed the door behind him, and I figured that was fine.

"As I said, your mom and I are going to be taking a break. I moved into the summer house. I don't know what's going to happen in the future, but that's something your mom and I will figure out. Natalie, this has nothing to do with you."

I snorted as Tanner just growled.

"I promise. This has been a long time coming. I haven't been okay with some of the things she has been doing recently, and that's not something you need to know more about unless you want to. And I know this is a lot right now. I love you, Natalie. You're my only daughter. My child. I've always loved you. And I'm trying to respect your choices, but I think my burdens altered how I saw things. I'm sorry."

"How is this happening?" I asked, my hands shaking.

"It's not you, Natalie. Maybe the way we both reacted was the final straw, but I didn't like who I was becoming. And that's on me. Later, we can all talk. When I'm not throwing things at you. I can already tell it's a lot. But I didn't think a phone call or a letter would suffice for this."

"You and Mom are getting a divorce?"

My dad nodded. "Likely. I don't think taking a break is going to cut it. But that's on us. I'll always be your father." He let out a shaky laugh. "And, apparently, a grandfather. I knew it could—and likely would—happen. It's not like you're fifteen anymore."

"No, I'm not."

"I'd still like to be able to come to your graduation. And hear what your plans are." He looked around the house. "What about after this? I don't want to presume that you two will be living together, but have you figured out where you're going to go?"

I met Tanner's gaze, and he gave me a shrug, telling me that it was up to me.

"I'm using one of my trust funds to buy a small house with Tanner." I still couldn't believe Tanner was okay with that, but we were doing it for the baby.

"That's great. If that gets too difficult with legal things, let me know. I'll help."

"Dad," I whispered.

"It's my first grandbaby. I didn't expect this, and had my head up my ass. But I'm here now. Anyway, I'll leave you two be. We'll talk soon."

"I don't know what to say, Dad."

"You don't have to say anything yet. Just know I'm here if you need me. Always. Oh, did you get the inspection?"

"It's on the list. We're just at the beginning stages. They accepted the offer."

"You should use Mark."

"I planned on it." *There* was the father I remembered, the one always trying to help me with what he was good at.

"I know you're an adult, and you can handle things. But with graduation, I guess finals coming up, and the baby…let me help."

"Dad."

"Please. Let me help."

"This is my first time buying a house, too. I'm using some of my savings for the down payment," Tanner put in. "I'd like help in making sure we're doing it right if you're offering."

I looked at Tanner and fell that much more in love with him. My father was trying, and Tanner was letting him in.

My dad smiled for the first time in so long, I realized I'd missed it. "Okay. Anything you want. I'm here. And, Tanner? I never once thought that you were trying to take advantage of my daughter. At least, with the house." He blushed. "I might have thought a couple of things at first because I was an asshole—and probably still am."

Tanner snorted. "You wouldn't be the first person to think that."

Dad's lips quirked into a smile. "That I'm an asshole? Or that you're taking advantage of my baby?"

"Dad."

"I was thinking taking advantage, but the asshole thing…you never know." Tanner just laughed, and my dad joined in.

"Let me help with the paperwork and make sure you're doing it right because this is your first time. And then maybe I will feel like I'm actually doing something."

I started crying then, and both men looked as if they were out of their depths. I sighed, stood, and hugged my dad hard.

"Thank you. I will call you to help with the paperwork. I promise."

"Good. I love you."

"I love you, too."

Dad left after shaking Tanner's hand, and I felt as if I had just been hit by a two-by-four.

"My parents are getting a divorce."

"Is it wrong that I'm glad your mother wasn't here?" Tanner asked dryly.

I turned to look at him and snorted. "No, I'm kind of with you there. I know we're closing on the house near the end of the summer, and we have a bunch of things to go over, but I think my dad is making sure we don't get screwed in the paperwork. That's probably a good thing."

"Considering the man knows how to make money, I'm sure he knows how to spend it wisely, too. At least, I hope so."

"So you're okay with it?"

"Of course, I'm okay with it. We're jumping into this headfirst over and over again without being able to look backward and realize what we're doing. I'm fine with it." He cupped my face and kissed me again. "I don't know what I'd do without you, Natalie. I'm not talking about the house. Or the money. I just don't know what I'd do without you."

"I love you," I blurted, surprising myself. I hadn't thought I'd be the one to say it first, but I couldn't stop myself. I wanted him to know. I was tired of holding back because I was afraid he might leave. He wasn't going to leave. So, I just needed to open myself and do it.

His eyes widened for an instant, and I was so afraid he would break me. Instead, he smiled. "I love you, too. Damn it, I should have said it a long time before this."

"I guess we both should have. That means you're here for the baby and me."

"I fell for you long before I kissed you, long before the baby."

"Really?" Warmth slid over the ice within me, and I felt like I was breaking a bit, but in the best way possible.

"I fell for you the moment I saw you. The moment I knew you couldn't be mine. And then we went off in different directions, trying to live the lives we thought we needed to lead. And yet, we found each other no matter what. You're mine, Natalie. I know we started this relationship backwards, but we're finding our way forwards. I love you with every ounce of my being. To the depths of my soul. You might be marrying a former stripper, and an Air Force brat, but I'm marrying a princess."

I snorted. "You may be a former stripper, but I'm not a princess. I've never been."

"You're mine. Does that count?"

Tears flowed again, and I leaned forward and kissed him, needing him.

"We really should've just said this before," I whispered, and he laughed.

"You know people keep telling me that just saying what you're feeling and what you're thinking opens things and makes it easier. But that is so much easier said than done. What if you had said no? What if you had walked away?"

Tears fell again, and I rose to wipe a single tear

from his cheek. "I wouldn't have walked away. I was so afraid you would."

"Next time, we talk to each other."

I laughed. "Next time, we don't do things in the wrong order."

He laughed again and then leaned forward to take my lips. I was lost. This time, in the best way possible.

Twenty

Tanner

My arm lay protectively over Natalie's stomach, the two of us lying naked in her bed as the sun rose. I was exhausted, not having slept the night before. To say that things were busy would be an understatement. While I wasn't working long nights anymore, finals were kicking our asses, but we were almost finished. We were also in the process of packing—mostly her house since their lease was up soon. We had other boxes of baby things at my place since I had more room, but we were all set for the small house that we would be closing on in a few weeks.

I still couldn't believe that we were doing this. That she loved and trusted me enough to let me be part of her life.

I had always looked at Natalie as someone I knew I would care about, despite the fact we were two different people. She didn't see that. She saw only me—sometimes even before I did.

I didn't like to think long and hard about who I was or where I came from or wax philosophical about who I could be.

However, Natalie made me do that.

I'd thought my life would be something entirely different. That we would walk away from each other after teasing one another for a few moments, and she would forget all about me. She would marry a rich husband, have cute little babies, and be happy.

I hadn't realized that her apparent happiness had only been a façade at times. That while her pain and past might be completely different than mine, we shared an edge.

Now, she was mine.

And I would be damned if I let her go.

I might still feel as if I wanted to run sometimes and act like an idiot who couldn't ever be good enough for her, but I was trying to be better.

Natalie moaned and snuggled closer. I swallowed hard, my dick pressing against her backside.

"Good morning to you," she mumbled, her voice soft and sweet.

I snorted. "Ignore him. You're exhausted."

"It's really hard to ignore the steel pole pressing into my butt. But sure, I can try if you'd like."

"I love when you talk dirty to me."

"If that is talking dirty, I need to get better and practice more."

"I think you're doing just fine."

"Whatever you say. I know that we need to head out and do some more packing and meet with the rest of the roommates later, but I'm enjoying myself just lying here." She stretched in my arms, her breasts pushing towards my face. I leaned down and sucked a nipple into my mouth, making her groan.

"Seriously, good morning."

I mumbled and kept looking at her, needing her.

"I love how you taste." I moved my hand between her legs. She arched into me as her hand wrapped around my cock. I swallowed hard, pumping into her gently, both of us acting as if this were just a typical morning. And it could be.

Somehow, these would be my mornings.

Me. Tanner Hagen.

Natalie cupped my face and frowned.

"You've got that look that means you're not with me."

I shook my head and kissed her again as I slid my hand over her clit. She moaned, her body shaking. "I'm always with you."

"Good, continue to be with me."

As we both showered love on one another and sent each other over the edge, I knew that she would be mine forever. I might not have expected her, but she was it for me.

I would never let her go.

Afterwards, we both lay there holding each other, and I sighed. "We should go shower and clean each other up. We have things to do."

"You're right. We may be nearly done with all of our school stuff before graduation, but that doesn't mean we can spend a lazy day in bed."

"That does sound like a dream, though."

I kissed her again, and then we both went to take a shower. It took longer than it should have because I made sure she was perfectly clean all over and then watched as she dressed.

She had on a maternity dress now and frowned.

"What is it?"

"When did my belly get this big? My ankles are the size of dinner plates."

I shook my head, getting hard again just looking at

her. She'd always been able to do that to me, even before we'd kissed the first time, and I swore I was the bad bet. "That's a lie."

"It doesn't feel like one. I'm really pregnant, Tanner."

I looked at her then, frowning. "You're right. You've been pregnant for what? Seven months now?"

"Nearly."

"You are *really* pregnant. I like the look on you."

She glared at me. "That means we've been together for those seven months."

I froze, doing the math. I'd never been with anyone that long. "Really?"

"More like five months. Maybe. I don't know when our anniversary will be."

I just smiled at her as I zipped my jeans. "If we think about the conception date as our anniversary, that could work."

"You mean our wham, bam, thank you, ma'am?"

I scowled. "Excuse me? There was nothing wham or bam about it."

"You have taught me that we can go fast, slow, hard, soft, or anything in between and still make it worthwhile."

"Damn straight." I wrapped my hand around the back of her neck and kissed her hard. "You should rest today." I'd always been a little overprotective when it came to Natalie, but these days, I was going full tilt.

"I have packing to do."

"We're going to have those weeks without the lease on this place. Are you ready to live with me at the guys' house?"

"At some point, I think there'll be eight of us living there. But we'll make it work. Pacey's house is ridiculously large."

"Yes, but we can make it work."

"We're doing this."

I studied her face, then leaned forward and kissed her again. "I love you, Natalie. Yes, we're doing this."

She brushed my hair from my face and smiled. "We wasted so much time being afraid."

I swallowed hard. "I don't know. Maybe fear is what we needed. So we knew that this was worth it."

"Given our relationship means we're making up our anniversary date because we didn't go on a date until I was nearing my second trimester tells me that maybe we did this backwards, but we're doing it right now."

"That sounds good to me."

I kissed her again, and then my phone rang. I frowned and pulled it out of my pocket, sighing. "It's my mom."

"Answer."

I shook my head. "I still haven't truly forgiven her for everything that happened."

"Your mom tried her best. If anything, you should do it for your brother."

"You're right."

"Answer. I'll be here if you need me." She took my hand, and I sighed and answered.

"Hey, Mom."

"Hi there. Can you come and help me?"

Ice slid through my veins, and I swallowed hard. "What's wrong?"

Mom let out a breath. "I love you, baby. I'm so sorry for how things worked out, and I'm going to fix it. I need your help picking up a few more things. Your brother and I are moving out."

I stiffened, a kernel of hope taking root. "You're leaving him?"

"Yes. Finally. I should've done it a long time ago. We can talk more in person. I can't fit everything in my van, and I could use your help."

"You're on the lease, Mom. Not him."

"You're right. But I need a clean break. He's not here right now, and I could really use the help. Please, Tanner. I know I should have left him ages ago, but I'm doing it now. Please."

"Of course. I'll be right there."

Natalie looked up at me, her eyes wide. "Wow. She's leaving him?"

"Yes, and moving out, apparently. I don't know what her plan is, but I'll ask her when I'm there. Is it okay if you stay here?"

"I want to help, though," Natalie said, frowning.

"If he shows up, I don't want to have to protect you, my mother, and my brother. Plus, you can't lift anything. You're like eighteen months pregnant."

She flipped me off, even as she smiled. "Watch it, mister. And, of course. I'll do some packing here—I promise I won't lift anything," she added at my frown.

"Just be safe." I kissed her hard. "Please."

My heart raced, and I knew I needed to get to my mother fast, just in case Jared came back. I didn't want to leave Natalie behind. Only I knew she couldn't go with me to this.

"I'll be here when you get back. Or I'll be at your place where I'll cook something for everybody. I'm in the mood to nest, and since we can't do that here, it might need to be at the guys' house."

"Whatever you need. I will be there."

She rolled her eyes, kissed me again, and pushed me out of the room. "Go. They need you."

I swallowed hard, my heart pounding, and made my way to my truck.

Traffic was a bitch, and it took me longer than I

wanted to get there, but I scrambled out as soon as I saw my mom ducking a fist.

"You stupid bitch! You don't get to leave me."

Anger slammed into me, my whole body shaking, and my muscles clenched.

Jared stood over my mother in front of the tiny home that had once been mine and shouted down at her. Cody hid behind the bushes, his phone in his hands. He looked up at me, tears streaming down his face, and I knew I was probably going to kill someone. My little brother had a handprint on his cheek, a bright red mark on his pale skin, and I saw red.

I was going to rip Jared's arms from his body and beat him with them. Only Natalie's voice stopped me. She might not have been here in person, but I could hear her, nonetheless.

If I kill this man, or even get in a fight and go to jail, I will lose her. I will lose Natalie. The baby. I'll lose everyone.

I moved forward and did my best not to fracture everything I had tried to build. "Get your fucking hands off her," I growled, my voice low. I gripped Jared's wrist as he went for another swing and pulled him back.

"You fucker. You've always wanted to ruin this. You didn't like that I stepped into your daddy's shoes. Get over it. I'm the man of the house now. You're not."

"I don't know what the hell is going on in that

twisted brain of yours, but that's my mother. My brother. This is *my* family. You don't get to step into my dad's shoes. You're barely half the man he was. Less. My dad was a fucking hero. He died for our country. What have you done? Gotten drunk and beat up on women? No. Fuck you. Get away from here."

"Don't you talk to me, boy," he growled and tried to hit me again. I ducked the blow and slammed my fist into the man's stomach.

"Mom, call the cops."

"Cody has my phone," she whispered before letting out a shaky breath. "I told him to get safe. I'm coming, Cody. I'm coming."

"I'm calling, Mom!" Cody shouted from the bushes.

"You bitch," Jared growled, and I shoved him away when I caught sight of the blade in his hand. He swiped at me with the knife, then looked down at his hand and growled.

"Look what you made me do. I don't want to kill you. I just don't want you here."

"Tanner! Watch out!" my mom called, and I jumped out of the way of the knife again, nearly plowing into my mother.

I stood in front of her, protecting her, praying that Cody would stay put.

"The cops are coming," Cody screamed, and Jared narrowed his eyes.

"Fine, fuck all of you. Fuck this. I'm done." He closed the knife, stuck it into his pocket, and ran. I could have chased him. I could have held him down to make sure he stayed for when the cops arrived. Instead, I held my mother as she bawled, her tears soaking my shirt, and we fell onto the porch, me holding her as my little brother barreled into us. We sat there as a family. When the cops came, they told us they would search for Jared.

They believed us when we said we were the victims.

But I wondered what the hell we were going to do and how much longer it would take until I could get home.

To Natalie. To my future and not the past. It seemed I still threatened to break everything over and over again.

Twenty-One

Natalie

I put tape on the last of the boxes and sighed. This was it. We were moving. After over a year in this home, four years of living with most of the girls, we weren't going to be roommates anymore. Yes, we had a few weeks together with the guys in their house, but we'd be moving on soon, and everything would change yet again.

"I can't believe how quickly we packed everything up." Mackenzie held her clipboard close to her chest as she looked around the living room where we'd shared countless dinners and girls' nights.

I grinned as I looked down at her clipboard and shook my head, memories hitting hard.

"Is that the same one you used for the list to get us in here?"

"Of course," she answered, rolling her eyes. "What else would I do?"

"At least, you're consistent." Elise winked as I grinned.

Nessa laughed from the other side of the towers of boxes, her eyes full of happiness and joy, something that had been missing for far too long. "Are you going to meet us at the restaurant?"

I nodded. "I want to wait here for Tanner, and then we'll meet you and the guys at Dillon's bar."

"I love that we call it Dillon's bar." Elise snorted. "It irks his brothers just enough for a little brotherly competition."

"We do call it Dillon's bar, but anytime Dillon uses Aiden's recipes, we call it Aiden's food, so we're not taking sides," I joked. The baby kicked, and I groaned, putting my hand over my stomach. "I think the kicks are getting harder."

Mackenzie smiled and leaned forward to put her hand on my belly. Only my core group of eight were allowed to touch me without permission, and even then, they could see it in my eyes. "The baby's getting stronger. It only makes sense that would happen."

"I still can't believe this," I whispered. "It still feels so strange that I'm sitting here about to have a baby."

"With the love of your life," Elise added and reached forward. I grinned and helped her place her hand on the right part of my stomach. "Wow, they *are* strong kicks."

"The strongest."

Nessa leaned forward. "Look at you, acting like an Earth mother."

I rolled my eyes. "Not so much Earth mother. More like tired mom. I cannot believe the baby's going to be here in only a few short weeks."

"I feel like we just found out you were pregnant," Mackenzie said dryly.

"That's how I feel. Tanner and I are barely figuring out how we want to spend the rest of our lives, and we're about to have another life to hold and cherish and grow with along the way."

"You guys don't do things in half-measures. Not the princess or the party boy stripper," Nessa added with a wink.

"I can't believe you didn't tell us that he was a stripper." Elise pointed her finger at me.

I blushed. "It wasn't my place. Plus, I didn't want you all thinking about him stripping for anyone but me."

"I don't know what I would do if Dillon wanted to

do that," Elise said before grinning. "Okay, maybe I'd like it."

"Just for you. I'm a little more possessive," Mackenzie teased.

"I'm possessive, too. Tanner might've shaken his hips for some people, but he always came home to me. At least he has for the past few months."

"See? That's sweet. And now this is going to be the last week we ever sleep under this roof." Nessa sighed. "Not that we're sleeping much here these days with so many boxes. We've all pretty much decided to sleep at the guys' house more often than not."

Elise moved forward and grabbed all our hands. "Tomorrow night, then. We still have the beds, we can make sure we have a set of sheets. We'll all sleep here, or even in the living room. I don't know. One last girls' night."

I looked at them and swallowed hard. "One last girls' night."

We all hugged, laughed, cried, and then I was alone, the rest of them needing to head out to their various appointments and to see their guys. All I wanted was for Tanner to check in with me so I could make sure he was okay. He hadn't texted, and it worried me. But I knew he would get back to me soon. He had to.

Everything would be okay. We were starting our next phase.

I held my belly and looked down at the baby. "Daddy will be home soon. And then we can get you something to eat. I am craving strawberry jam, and I have a feeling that's all you. It has nothing to do with me."

I yawned, shook my head, and then lay down on the couch. The movers would be here in a week to finish everything, and this couch was mine--one that would go to my new home with Tanner. First, though, it would go to a storage unit. We had all decided that if we were able, we would use storage units for some of our stuff because it would be a little ridiculous to try and fit everything into Pacey's house, regardless of how big it was.

I yawned again, lay my head on a pillow, and was out before I knew it, images of Tanner on my mind.

I woke coughing, my eyes burning, wondering what the hell was going on.

I sat up and looked around, choking on a scream. Smoke billowed from the kitchen area where the fuse box was, and I held back a shout.

There hadn't been a storm. Lightning didn't trip the fuse box again. But there was a fire. An actual fire.

I saw flames from the other side of the house and dropped to my hands and knees, the smoke far too thick above me. I remembered that as long as I stayed low, I could make it out. I needed to make it out. My phone was still in my hand, and I shook, knowing I needed to call 911, to call Tanner, to do something.

I needed to get out. Only I couldn't think. The smoke was too thick, and I kept coughing. A shadow moved towards me, and I shrieked, wondering if I was seeing things.

Only it wasn't just a shadow.

Jared hovered over me, grinning even as he coughed.

"Stupid bitch. You should have left us alone, just like that little asshole of yours."

This was Jared. Had he started the fire? What was he doing here? Was this all a dream? I couldn't think. He kept talking, and then there was a grunt and a shout and the sound of something hitting the floor. I couldn't figure out what was going on, and I couldn't focus on Jared. I needed to get out of the house.

I tried to crawl away. My baby needed to be okay.

I coughed again as strong arms lifted me. I tried to reach out, tried to tell whoever held me that I needed to save my baby. The person carried me out of the house, and I tried to cover my mouth, to protect my lungs and my child.

The baby. The baby had to be okay.

"You're fine. You're going to be fine. The ambulance is on its way," Tanner whispered from my side, and I looked up at him as he fell to the ground, holding me in his arms. I wept.

"Tanner." My throat hurt, my eyes burned, but this was Tanner. *My* Tanner. He had me.

"I'm fine."

I saw a burn on his cheek, his beautiful skin marred, and there was soot on his ear and his chin.

"Can you breathe?"

I coughed but nodded. "I can breathe."

"Good, I love you so fucking much."

"How? How did you get here? What happened?"

"Don't speak. Save your throat."

I gave him a pleading look, and he sighed, holding me close. "I was coming over to get you. I saw the flames and ran inside to find you."

I scowled at him.

"I know it was stupid, but the paramedics weren't here yet. Nor were the firefighters."

As the sirens got louder, I looked up, and everyone started moving all at once as soon as they parked near us.

"You saved us," I whispered, my hands on him and on my belly.

"I'm so sorry," he replied. I looked over to see that

a firefighters had run in and pulled out another body. Jared lay shaking, coughing into his hands. It seemed he had almost died from his own fire—if that's truly what'd happened. I couldn't rationalize it all right now.

Maybe one day it would make sense. But for now, I just let the paramedics give me oxygen, monitor my vitals, check the baby, and hoped everything would be okay.

As Tanner held me, I looked over my shoulder and saw the firefighters spraying down half the house.

It had been old, rickety, and still held a lot of our things.

Now, it was broken.

Everything was broken.

I wasn't sure what to think, so I didn't.

I told myself I would think later and just let Tanner hold me, praying that the baby would be okay.

Twenty-Two

Tanner

The sun shone through the blinds of my bedroom, and unlike the previous morning, I wasn't thinking of how nice everything felt against me. Instead, I clung to Natalie and never wanted to let go.

She had finally fallen asleep only a couple of hours prior, the sun just rising. We had spent most of the day yesterday at the hospital, checking her vitals and those of the baby. They both seemed healthy and would be fine. And while that's what they told us, I hadn't actually come to believe it yet. It felt as if I had almost lost the love of my life again. We'd almost lost our baby. Natalie had gone to the floor quickly, had moved fast, and hadn't breathed in as much smoke as she thought. She *had* panicked while trying to get out, though. That was why she had gotten dizzy; not because of the smoke.

She would be fine. We would all be fine. Even if it took me longer than I cared to admit to finally let her go at the hospital the day before.

"You're grumbling," she muttered against me, and I froze, the baby kicking my hand.

"Sorry, did I wake you?"

"No, I couldn't sleep. And we're hungry."

I kissed the back of her neck and rolled out of bed, walking around to help her up.

"I forgot how high your bed was," she said as she sat on the edge of the mattress and traced her fingers along my jaw. I had a bandage on my face. The numbing cream made it so it didn't hurt that much, but I knew it would soon. My cheekbone had gotten burned slightly, and I would probably carry the scar for the rest of my life, but that was fine. It would be a reminder of what I could've lost. What *we* could've lost. And I thought I needed the reminder.

"I could've lost you," Natalie whispered.

I shook my head. "That's what I was thinking."

"We didn't lose each other. That's all that matters."

"I can't believe Jared came back to try to hurt you," I grumbled.

I helped her out of bed, and we both rushed downstairs in our pajamas. I noticed the others were already up before she could say anything back.

"Oh, good, none of us is sleeping," Nessa said as she scooted closer to Miles on the couch. I sat down, Natalie on my lap, and the eight of us just rested, none of us speaking for a moment as we tried to come to terms with what had happened.

"The insurance person, the fire inspector, and other people will be at the house today," Mackenzie said after a moment, looking down at her phone. "The landlord isn't coming. I don't think they care. They're going to get money out of the deal anyway."

"And it looks like we're out a few of our things," Elise said before she looked over at us there. "Not that it matters. The important paperwork is all safe, as are a lot of our memory things. We mostly just lost everything from the kitchen and anything we had boxed up in the mudroom. That's what the water hit most because the fire didn't get the other side of the house."

"That's good. I'm glad that anything important that could've been hurt had already been moved to this place or to storage." Natalie looked up at me and kissed my chin. "Stop feeling guilty."

"I'm going to feel guilty for a long fucking time," I grumbled.

"If I don't get to feel guilty about my dad, you don't get to feel that way about Jared," Dillon growled.

I looked up at that and remembered the horror that Dillon and Elise had gone through because of Dillon's dad. I swallowed hard.

"Why do people who think they're part of our family keep trying to hurt us?" I asked, unaware I'd even voiced the question until everyone went even more silent.

"They're not ours, though," Natalie whispered. "The people that we care about are in this room or close to it. Dillon's family loves him, and some of them were made and found, not blood-related. Yet, still, they are his family."

"They're your family, too," Dillon said, a small smile on his face.

"I'm finally getting along with my parents. But for a while, I thought that Dillon's family would be my only family." Elise shook her head.

"We don't need to talk about my family," Pacey chimed in with hollow laughter.

"I have my dad and Everly and her family, but you guys are it for me, too," Nessa added.

"We have blood family, but we also have the one we made," Miles said after a moment.

"We are not responsible for the actions of those who hate us. Not for those who think they know better than us, either." I looked at Miles and Nessa, at the rest of them, and nodded tightly.

"It still doesn't make it right."

"No, but that's on him," Natalie said. "Our memories are safe. And, yes, we lost all our kitchen things and a few boxes of clothes, but we're safe. The baby's safe. All that can be replaced." She let out a shaky breath, and I wiped away her tear. "And, honestly, Jared is safe."

I glared. "Really?"

"If he had died because you pulled me out of the fire instead of him, you would've felt guilt. Yes, Jared deserved to be hurt and deserves to be locked up. But he didn't deserve to die. Nobody does. We can't put that on our souls. So, here we are. A family. All under one roof."

Pacey laughed. "The more, the merrier."

"So, I guess all eight of us will be living here for the next month or so?" Mackenzie asked as she looked around at everyone.

My arms tightened around Natalie's waist. "Looks like. We can store a lot of stuff in the basement or the attic. Or even Sanders' room."

"Let's not call it that." Mackenzie twisted her lips, and I snorted.

"How about the spare room?"

"That works for me," Pacey added. "Of course, if we just want to stay here forever, we could always make it the nursery." He winked.

Natalie laughed, and the sound was so joyous that I calmed. Finally. For the first time in over twenty-four hours, I was calm.

My mother and brother were safe at my aunt's house and would soon be moving into another home of their own. They would be free from Jared, and he would hopefully be locked up for a while.

We were all finding our own paths somehow, making things work. In the long run, all that truly mattered was that we had found our family. We were making it. While we might not be able to look back on our four years here—especially the last two together—without some painful memories, I hoped that the fond ones, the ones of joy, and thoughts of us being together were the ones that mattered.

"I can't believe how many godparents our baby's going to have," Natalie said after a moment when everyone else was speaking amongst themselves.

I looked down at her, and Miles cheered. "Yes. Though I get to be the best godparent, right? We all know that it's my turn. We'll alternate with the other kids."

"Other kids? Is there something I need to know?" Nessa asked with a wince.

Miles blustered. "I just mean, we can alternate between the four of us. We'll be their child's godparents, and then they can be Pacey and Mackenzie's kids' godparents, and then for Dillon and Elise, and so on."

"So you're saying that we're all going to have kids and get married and have a big future together?" Nessa asked, and Miles blushed to the tips of his ears. "I'm not *not* saying it."

She kissed him hard on the mouth, and we all laughed. Natalie leaned into me. "I think that sounds great. We can put in some spares like other family members. Though even as we all make friends and start new lives with new jobs and homes and neighborhoods and whatnot, it's the eight of us."

"That sounds like a plan to me," Pacey said, and I kissed the top of Natalie's head. "Soon, there'll be nine of us, so I guess we should make sure we all remain a family. Even if we're not all living under the same roof."

The others held up their coffee cups, and we did the same. We toasted to our future, one where we might not know everything that was going to come, but where we could try. We could pretend.

Or maybe not pretend because we'd worked for this. This was the future we wanted. The people we wanted in our lives. I had the one person I'd never thought to have, even though I'd almost lost her because of my stupidity and my hatred of another. Still, she was mine.

I'd fallen in love with Natalie Blake, the princess, the girl who wasn't for me. Yet, she was mine.

And, thankfully, I was hers.

Epilogue

Natalie

Four years later—

"You know, even though I only technically lived here for a month, I feel like this could be my second home." I looked over at Tanner as he led me inside the large home on University Row. It had been four years since we had left Pacey's house, all eight of us ready to embark on our new futures. Four years in which everything changed, yet the feeling of peace and family remained.

I looked up at my husband and grinned. He just rolled his eyes and kissed the top of my head.

"I'm pretty sure that last year you stayed here more than you did at your house. I'm just saying."

"Mom, Mom," Corinne exclaimed from the living room. "It's us!" She pointed at a framed photo on the mantel, and tears sprang to my eyes.

"Of course, she's crying. Of course, she's crying." Tanner muttered under his breath as he led me forward and moved to pick up our little girl. Corinne wrapped her arms around his neck, and I smiled up at my family.

The last four years hadn't been easy. Finishing grad school, working on internships, and landing our new jobs meant that we were exhausted most days and hadn't had much time for ourselves. We were making it work for the three of us, though.

We were a family, and thanks to the Montgomerys, we had childcare and great people to work with.

And, indeed, on the mantel were images and photos taken over the past six years. Some when we were still in school, all learning to be with one another and finding out who each of us was—others with all of our newfound families.

"You're here!" Mackenzie exclaimed as she walked into the living room, looking sexy as ever. She wore a red dress that showed off her curves and sparkly red heels that matched mine. The fact that all four girls would be wearing the same heels made me laugh. We didn't know why we had decided to do it. It'd just happened. Since it made us feel closer even though we only saw one another a couple of times a month—not including the multiple phone calls each day—I loved it.

"Of course, we're here," I said as I hugged my best friend close. Mackenzie kissed my cheek and then moved away as Elise waddled in. She was heavily pregnant, her ring finger bare because she wore her wedding ring around her neck.

"Don't look at me. Why did I decide to wear these shoes?"

I winced. "Because they look cute. But I still can't believe you're wearing heels. At least they're the kitten version."

"That's what I said," Dillon grumbled as he forced his wife into a seat. "Seriously. Stop standing. The fact that you're wearing fucking heels while pregnant is annoying the hell out of me."

"My fingers swelled because of the meds, not because of the pregnancy. Just stop."

He scowled, kissed her lips, and then plucked Corinne from my husband's arm. "Sorry for cursing in front of you."

"It's okay, Uncle Dillon. Daddy curses a lot. But Mommy curses more."

I rolled my eyes and shook my head. "From the mouths of babes."

"I can't wait," Elise said as she rubbed her belly. "This is so exciting. All of us back together."

"And we're going to a bar!" Corinne cried, clapping her hands.

"You know, I think we're teaching our daughter about these things a little too young," Tanner whispered as he held me to his side. I inhaled his scent, falling that much more in love with him. Seriously, every time I was with him, my hormones went nuts. I was ready to have another baby, one where we might be a little more planned and put together this time. Though I didn't know if he was ready. Given the way he growled at me every time he looked at me, he might be ready to practice for another one.

I leaned into him, kissed him hard on the mouth, and ran my hand over the burn on his cheek. The scar was slowly fading, but he wasn't going to get plastic surgery to fix anything that remained. He wanted the memory. Jared was gone, still in jail, and he would be for a long time to come. He had charges for illegal weapons, drugs, and battery, arson, and attempted murder. We'd never have to see him again.

Tanner's mother and little brother lived close to us, and we saw them weekly. Things were going well. Finally.

"I'm here, I'm here," Pacey said as he walked in, leaning heavily on his cane.

He looked debonair with it. As if he'd just walked off a Regency romance set.

"I still can't believe you broke your foot on a bicycle," Tanner said with a sigh.

"They say it's like riding a bike, but I don't really believe it."

"You fell off a stationary bike and broke your ankle." Mackenzie rolled her eyes. "Seriously, how does that even happen?"

"I don't want to talk about it," he growled, then came and sat down next to Elise.

"Oh, good, you can sit with me while I'm heavily pregnant. You're more of a dork than I am."

"Did someone say dork?" Miles asked as he walked in, Nessa at his side. Nessa looked radiant, fresh off her new book tour. It looked like she was on top of the world.

The two of them had gotten married soon after Tanner and I had, and I knew that they were living a life that neither of them had planned. The *New York Times* bestselling author status looked good on Nessa, and I knew she was nervous about her next book. But things were working out well, and she was still teaching.

Everything had changed these last four years, but here we were, in a reunion of sorts with just the eight of us. Nine if you included Corinne.

We had lost our friend at the beginning of our friendship, and I missed Corinne every single day. However, every time our little girl laughed just the right way, it reminded me of Corinne. Hence why our daughter shared her name. It had been Tanner's idea, and we had asked Elise, Mackenzie, and Nessa if they minded.

There had been lots of tears, but in the end, it had been the perfect name for our little girl. The one who had surprised us and made us a family in the way we always should have been. She had nudged us into the future we now had, and I wouldn't change any of that for the world.

We had a future, hope. We were a family.

The eight of us had been roommates once, but we were so much more than that now. We were family. We were what we had made.

Tanner handed me a flute of champagne as Elise took her sparkling cider, the same as Corinne, and we clinked glasses.

"To family," Pacey said. I looked up at Tanner, then at Corinne in his arms, and grinned.

"To family."

WANT TO READ A SPECIAL BONUS EPILOGUE FEATURING NATALIE & TANNER? CLICK HERE!

Bonus Epilogue

Tanner

Six years after graduation—

"Shouldn't Dillon be cooking this?" I grumbled from the kitchen as Natalie waddled in. Her waddle was seriously the cutest thing ever—not that I would ever say that. I liked my balls, and I didn't want to have them lopped off if I said that to her face.

Corinne ran behind her and pulled out the chair to the kitchen island. "Here you go, Mom."

"Thank you, baby," Natalie said, her mouth twitching into a smile.

"She sure does like taking care of you," I said as I leaned down, kissed the top of Corinne's head, and then Natalie's cheek.

"She learned it from you." My wife grinned. "As for Dillon, he'll be here soon. As will Pacey. They'll help you cook. You just have to do all the prep work."

"I still feel cheated that Miles never has to cook."

"I mean, I don't do much cooking either. We both know that those cooking lessons Miles and I took never actually worked."

I rolled my eyes and kissed my wife again, then said hello to the twins by pressing my ear to Natalie's belly before tossing Corinne over my shoulder.

She let out a squeal and giggled as I set her on her feet. "Are they going to be here soon?"

I looked over at Natalie and smiled. "They will."

"And Aunt Elise and Uncle Dillon are bringing the babies?"

"They are."

"What about Uncle Cody?"

I laughed. "Cody and Mom will be here soon, too."

"As will my dad," Natalie said.

Cody and my mom lived two blocks down, and Cody had become fast friends with Corinne. Despite the age difference, they were more like siblings than uncle and niece. My mother was seeing a new guy, a great man I liked. He took care of her and worshiped the ground she walked on. He had asked me if he could marry her, and I had laughed and said, of course. It wasn't my job to hold her back. Still, it was nice to know that my mother would be happy.

We hadn't seen Natalie's mother since that fateful dinner. She had moved to the east coast back with her family and wanted nothing to do with us. She had never met Corinne, and I didn't plan on letting her meet the babies.

Natalie's dad, however, was the best grandfather he could be. Our friends' parents did their best to be group grandparents, as well as JC and his husband Zeke, but Natalie's dad was a fantastic grandad.

"They're here!" Corinne shouted, pulling me out of my thoughts.

She scrambled away to the door, and I looked at Natalie. "Don't let those onions burn."

"You know you're putting your life in my hands."

I smacked a kiss on her mouth and went to the front door. We had bought another house last year when we realized our family would be too big for the starter home. Between Natalie's job, our savings, and my new job as a lead architect at a small company, thanks to the Montgomerys' recommendation, we were doing okay. Corinne still spent time with the Montgomerys at their daycare, as did any of the children from my company since everybody was so close, and Corinne hadn't wanted to leave her friends behind. We made do.

Hell, we were doing better than making do.

I opened the door, and the rest of my family stood there, grinning at me.

I took two-year-old Julia from Dillon's arms and held her close as she kissed my cheek, right over my burn scar. All the babies tended to do that. It was as if they wanted to kiss my boo-boos better. I didn't mind. It just reminded me that we were a family, and somehow, I was the luckiest guy in the world.

"I love this house," Elise exclaimed as she hugged me tight and made her way in. Dillon slapped me on the back, took Julia back, and made room for the next set.

Mackenzie and Pacey walked in, and I looked down at baby Sean in Mackenzie's arms.

"He's gorgeous."

"He's finally sleeping, so we are going to put him in your nursery if that's okay."

"The crib's all set up."

"You sure you're okay with us using the twins' bed before they do?"

"You're family. Get up there."

Miles and Nessa walked in, baby Rachelle in Miles' arms. She had wide eyes and looked up at me as if she were still getting to know the world. Since she was only a month old, I figured that was probably the case.

"Thanks for coming. I know you guys must be exhausted."

"What is sleep?" Nessa asked as she hugged me tightly and then made her way in.

"I'm going to hold her for a bit, and then I'll go let her lay down next to Sean," Miles added as he squeezed my shoulder.

"Sounds like a plan."

I shut the door behind them and knew that my family and the rest of our extended families would be here soon. We were having a massive dinner with the group to celebrate babies, new jobs, and life.

I couldn't believe that this was my family. It felt like just yesterday that I was dancing up on stage, doing my best to hide who I was and making sure the world didn't see me.

Now, I was in a home that I owned with my wife. Soon, there would be three children amongst us—and my life would be forever changed.

JC and Zeke would be over for dessert and coffee later to visit with the babies and relax with us. JC had retired from stripping soon after I had, and Zeke had a clean bill of health. The honorary grandpas spoiled Corinne and couldn't wait to hold the twins.

As Natalie walked in, Corinne dancing around her, I looked between my friends and smiled.

Dillon had scampered off to the kitchen, hopefully

to finish cooking and make sure those onions hadn't burned, but when he came back out, I held Natalie close and looked around.

This was the life I'd never thought to have.

I had thought I was the bad bet. The bad decision. But I had been wrong.

Natalie had been the first good decision I had ever made, but not the last when it came to the family I loved.

I wasn't a man of many words, nor was I a man who often shared what I was feeling or thinking. But Natalie had proven that maybe I was wrong. Perhaps all I needed was to try harder.

So, I would. Eventually. But for now, I held my family close, listened as people spoke about their weeks and how things had changed in the past six years. And I breathed. Because for nearly a decade of my life—eight years now—I had been with these people. And I wouldn't change it for the world.

I kissed my wife, looked down at our daughter, and wondered how the hell I had gotten this lucky.

Then again, maybe I was allowed to believe that it just was. Because this was no longer pretend.

This was our choice, our life.

Our family.

And we were only getting started.

A Note from Carrie Ann Ryan

Thank you so much for reading **MY BAD DECISIONS!**

I loved writing this series so much and I honestly am so happy with how it turned out. Thank you for all of your love for this crew and don't worry, you might just see them pop up in other romances soon!

In the mood for more from Carrie Ann Ryan? Try the Wilder Brothers series with One Way Back to Me.

The On My Own Series:

Book 0.5: My First Glance
Book 1: My One Night
Book 2: My Rebound
Book 3: My Next Play
Book 4: My Bad Decisions

WANT TO READ A SPECIAL BONUS EPILOGUE FEATURING NATALIE & TANNER? CLICK HERE!

If you want to make sure you know what's coming next from me, you can sign up for my newsletter at www.CarrieAnnRyan.com; follow me on twitter at @CarrieAnnRyan, or like my Facebook page. I also have a Facebook Fan Club where we have trivia, chats, and other goodies. You guys are the reason I get to do what I do and I thank you.

Make sure you're signed up for my MAILING LIST so you can know when the next releases are available as well as find giveaways and FREE READS.

Happy Reading!

Also from Carrie Ann Ryan

The Montgomery Ink: Fort Collins Series:

Book 1: Inked Persuasion

Book 2: Inked Obsession

Book 3: Inked Devotion

Book 3.5: Nothing But Ink

Book 4: Inked Craving

Book 5: Inked Temptation

The Montgomery Ink Legacy Series:

Book 1: Bittersweet Promises

The Wilder Brothers Series:

Book 1: One Way Back to Me

Book 2: Always the One for Me

The Aspen Pack Series:

Book 1: Etched in Honor

Montgomery Ink:

Book 0.5: Ink Inspired
Book 0.6: Ink Reunited
Book 1: Delicate Ink
Book 1.5: Forever Ink
Book 2: Tempting Boundaries
Book 3: Harder than Words
Book 3.5: Finally Found You
Book 4: Written in Ink
Book 4.5: Hidden Ink
Book 5: Ink Enduring
Book 6: Ink Exposed
Book 6.5: Adoring Ink
Book 6.6: Love, Honor, & Ink
Book 7: Inked Expressions
Book 7.3: Dropout
Book 7.5: Executive Ink
Book 8: Inked Memories
Book 8.5: Inked Nights
Book 8.7: Second Chance Ink

Montgomery Ink: Colorado Springs

Book 1: Fallen Ink
Book 2: Restless Ink

Book 2.5: Ashes to Ink

Book 3: Jagged Ink

Book 3.5: Ink by Numbers

The Montgomery Ink: Boulder Series:

Book 1: Wrapped in Ink

Book 2: Sated in Ink

Book 3: Embraced in Ink

Book 4: Seduced in Ink

Book 4.5: Captured in Ink

The Gallagher Brothers Series:

Book 1: Love Restored

Book 2: Passion Restored

Book 3: Hope Restored

The Whiskey and Lies Series:

Book 1: Whiskey Secrets

Book 2: Whiskey Reveals

Book 3: Whiskey Undone

The Fractured Connections Series:

Book 1: Breaking Without You

Book 2: Shouldn't Have You

Book 3: Falling With You

Book 4: Taken With You

The Less Than Series:

Book 1: Breathless With Her

Book 2: Reckless With You

Book 3: Shameless With Him

The Promise Me Series:

Book 1: Forever Only Once

Book 2: From That Moment

Book 3: Far From Destined

Book 4: From Our First

The On My Own Series:

Book 1: My One Night

Book 2: My Rebound

Book 3: My Next Play

Book 4: My Bad Decisions

The Ravenwood Coven Series:

Book 1: Dawn Unearthed

Book 2: Dusk Unveiled

Book 3: Evernight Unleashed

Redwood Pack Series:

Book 1: An Alpha's Path

Book 2: A Taste for a Mate

Book 3: Trinity Bound

Book 3.5: A Night Away

Book 4: Enforcer's Redemption
Book 4.5: Blurred Expectations
Book 4.7: Forgiveness
Book 5: Shattered Emotions
Book 6: Hidden Destiny
Book 6.5: A Beta's Haven
Book 7: Fighting Fate
Book 7.5: Loving the Omega
Book 7.7: The Hunted Heart
Book 8: Wicked Wolf

The Talon Pack:

Book 1: Tattered Loyalties
Book 2: An Alpha's Choice
Book 3: Mated in Mist
Book 4: Wolf Betrayed
Book 5: Fractured Silence
Book 6: Destiny Disgraced
Book 7: Eternal Mourning
Book 8: Strength Enduring
Book 9: Forever Broken
Book 10: Mated in Darkness

The Elements of Five Series:

Book 1: From Breath and Ruin
Book 2: From Flame and Ash
Book 3: From Spirit and Binding

Book 4: From Shadow and Silence

The Branded Pack Series:

(Written with Alexandra Ivy)

Book 1: Stolen and Forgiven

Book 2: Abandoned and Unseen

Book 3: Buried and Shadowed

Dante's Circle Series:

Book 1: Dust of My Wings

Book 2: Her Warriors' Three Wishes

Book 3: An Unlucky Moon

Book 3.5: His Choice

Book 4: Tangled Innocence

Book 5: Fierce Enchantment

Book 6: An Immortal's Song

Book 7: Prowled Darkness

Book 8: Dante's Circle Reborn

Holiday, Montana Series:

Book 1: Charmed Spirits

Book 2: Santa's Executive

Book 3: Finding Abigail

Book 4: Her Lucky Love

Book 5: Dreams of Ivory

The Tattered Royals Series:

Book 1: Royal Line

Book 2: Enemy Heir

The Happy Ever After Series:

Flame and Ink

Ink Ever After

About the Author

Carrie Ann Ryan is the New York Times and USA Today bestselling author of contemporary, paranormal, and young adult romance. Her works include the Montgomery Ink, Redwood Pack, Fractured Connections, and Elements of Five series, which have sold over 3.0 million books worldwide. She started writing while in graduate school for her advanced degree in chemistry and hasn't stopped since. Carrie Ann has written over seventy-five novels and novellas with more in the works. When she's not losing herself in her emotional and action-packed worlds, she's reading as much as she can while wrangling her clowder of cats who have more followers than she does.

www.CarrieAnnRyan.com